ECONOMICS

ECONOMICS

STORIES BY FANNY HOWE

FLOOD EDITIONS CHICAGO 2002

Six of these stories were published in *The Boston Globe Magazine*. "The
Weather" was published as "The Right Thing" in *Ms Magazine* and *The
Best of Ms Magazine*. "Lotto" appeared in *Chicago Review* and "Gray"
in *Ploughshares* and *The Pushcart Prize XXV* (2001). The author extends
special thanks to Devin Johnston and to the Fanny Hurst Visiting Writer
Residency at Washington University.

CONTENTS

THE WEATHER

THE WHITE COUPLE who adopted the black child were not happy with what they got. Carol, the wife, had wanted a "mixed" female; John, the husband, had not really wanted another child at all. But, aside from being a social obligation, it was also a present for their daughter Jessica, who got a dog the year before. They named the baby Malcolm, a name they never would have used on a white boy, and took him home.

To social workers, Carol and John were the ideal adoptive couple. They owned their own house on the fringes of Boston. John was employed by the state college as an assistant professor of music; Carol did part-time work as a research assistant for a Harvard man. They were comfortable, clean, and socially aware.

"I just can't go through with another pregnancy," Carol had said, "but I don't want my daughter to be an only child either, the way I was."

Carol had pale blond hair that was cut straight below her ears. She wore horn-rimmed glasses. A wide, mobile mouth. With her bespectacled and balding husband, she shared a preoccupation with material order. Neither could tolerate chaos of any kind, not in their house nor in their community. Each aspired to social justice because it made good common sense. And to each the slogan "peace and freedom" made great sense, as it did to most comfortable people.

They drove the baby home in the heat of a June day. He was six months old already, and the foster parents who had raised him so far had described him as "easy." Malcolm lay on Carol's lap, not a big baby, his eyes fixed on her face. He wore a little blue suit and held his hands together. His eyes were round and alert for a baby, his nose flat, his lips dry and pink. Carol ran her hand across his soft curls.

"I hope we're doing the right thing," she said.

John's glasses flared in her direction. Sweat glistened along his pale red hairline. Heaps of cars fumed in traffic around them.

"We'll see," he said, as he always did, though his eyesight was very weak.

WHEN THEY GOT HOME, Jessica was seated on the front porch, waiting. A high-browed girl with long legs and red golden curls, she leaped up and down, thrilled with the baby. The dog, a sheepdog named Mozart, leaped about Carol's legs impatiently.

"Down, down!" Carol cried, lifting the baby high as they all trooped up into the house.

Their rooms were furnished in a modern, almost austere fashion—Danish stick furniture, glass-topped tables, bare floors polished with bowling-alley wax, and bright-colored throw rugs. All books were locked away, upstairs, in John's study.

They marched upstairs in a single file to the small room set aside for the baby. The walls and crib were white; the rug was a green shag. Already the dydee service had delivered the first batch, and cream for diaper rash sat in a jar with pins.

Carol laid the baby on his back on the changing table while Jessica and John flanked her, gaping.

"God, I hope I can remember how to do it," she was saying. "It better all come back to me, or else!"

She paused reverentially, for she never did anything in a hurry, and gazing out the window, said, "This is the way to do it. No pregnancy, no labor."

He began to thrash his legs up and down, and Carol directed her attention to his pants. He had made a mess.

"Oh God," she whispered, holding her nose, "I can't take it."

John took over as Carol moved away.

"What's wrong, Mom?"

"Nothing. It just takes getting used to."

Jessica stepped in to help her father. She went to the bathroom for a wet washcloth to clean the baby off, and after that she rubbed cream on his bottom.

"I'm sorry," sighed Carol. "I'll get over it, I'm sure."

BUT SHE NEVER DID. It was the first in a series of things she couldn't take about Malcolm. The second was his sex. Deep down, she didn't like boys or men. Raised by her mother alone, she was not used to the other sex. Even her husband was, at heart, a stranger, and not fully welcome, as her mother and daughter were, into the heart of her affections. He and she were held together by a similar outlook on society, and by Jessica. They kept out of each other's hair, delicately. While John tinkered, Carol organized women's groups, parent-teacher confrontations, summer programs for urban children, and pro-busing rallies.

Soon Carol gave John the main responsibility for raising Malcolm. John's only obligations included two or three courses in music theory; the rest of the time he worked on building a harpsichord. Carol felt that John, economically more privileged than she, should compensate for her losses as a child, when she was poor. When he was gliding, she was struggling. Luckily, his temperament was an obliging one. "Peace at any cost," was his motto.

So John assumed basic responsibility for Malcolm, while Carol continued to pour her spare energies into Jessica. She drove her to ballet lessons, swimming, and piano lessons; she took her to puppet shows and children's theater. She adored her daughter—but so did John, and he had come to question why Carol had insisted on adopting another child.

"For Jessica," she would insist.

And it was true that Jessica was enthralled by Malcolm. She carried him up and down stairs, from room to room, showed him how to work his toys, lay on the rug with him cooing, fed him, and changed him. He was at first "easy," as they were told he would be. But he grew robust very fast and by Christmas he was walking, climbing stairs, knocking things off tables, and throwing stuff around. In Carol's eyes, he was worse than their rambunctious sheepdog.

She hired babysitters for Malcolm when John was gone and Jessica at school, and sometimes on weekends when they went on family outings.

"Give me a break," she would say, "I just want a little time alone with you guys."

Jessica and John always conceded to Carol, but felt bad for leaving Malcolm behind. By this time, Malcolm had names for each member of the family—Jecca, Dada, and Momma. He had been taught these names by Jessica, and they stuck.

THERE WERE CERTAIN OCCASIONS when Carol would take Malcolm with her. These were invariably marches or meetings involving the issue of race. Boston was, at this time, obsessed with race. Blacks and whites could think of little else in the midst of such confusion and intensity. The national conflict over where to live—in the city, the county, or the suburbs—was magnified tenfold in this city where the sun never seems to shine.

For Carol, the decision to stay in the city—made years before—was founded on her political ideology, as was her adoption of Malcolm. With Malcolm, she could be conspicuously counted as a friend of the militants; he was her sword and her shield. So she took him with her to meetings on race matters, though never to the Stop & Shop in white Chestnut Hill. She was not oblivious to the hypocritical side of these actions, and for the first time in her life discovered she was not altogether good and righteous. She did not enjoy the discovery and went to a therapist to purge herself.

"I feel so guilty," she told the man. "Either I hate Malcolm, or I pity him. There's no in between. I even hate his name! It reminds me of cucumbers."

"But you gave him that name, didn't you," asked the man.

"Yes. For political reasons."

"Then that's something to feel guilty about. The rest is—well, something to deal with. I mean, it's very hard to control the feelings, but it can be done."

"I don't want to spend the rest of my life controlling my feelings."

"Well, what's the alternative?"

"I don't know, but I'll think of something."

She spent the rest of the afternoon at the public library, perusing books about child-rearing and problems with adoption. They offered no solutions, and she went out to the dreary February twilight, her mood much like the weather. She gazed around her at the city with a sudden surge of disgust.

"Maybe if we move to Florida, or California, the problem will disappear," she figured. "Maybe it has something to do with this city, with its endless racism."

Driving home, she envisioned the family in a new environment, but her spirits did not lift.

"Or maybe," she went on, "I should just split, with Jessica. John can have Malcolm."

THERE ARE CERTAIN THOUGHTS that arise, conscious calculations of great force, that stun the thinker. Carol was shocked at herself for being so scheming. But if it was a hard task controlling the emotions, it was a harder one controlling the thoughts. Anything could happen in the head. And her head was exposing itself to her spirit as completely out of kilter with her public image. She could casually dispose of half her family without a second thought.

She had reached that moment in life when either one's mask becomes, irrevocably, one's face; or when the mask is thrown away as useless and one stands, frankly flawed, before the crowd. She could, she knew, continue as she was, pretending to love the little boy in her house and thereby, over time, prove herself a martyr to the cause of racial integration. On the other hand, she could actually do the opposite—liberate herself from her husband and her home, and with her daughter make a fresh start as a completely selfish person. At least, for a little while she imagined she could.

FREED BY HER KNOWLEDGE of her own imperfection, she began to experiment with the flaws. She would not let John touch her in bed, on those rare occasions when he made a sensual suggestion, saying that he was not necessary to her survival, she could live without sex and not miss it, and that she would prefer sleeping in a room of her own. He did not protest.

But the main heat of her effort went into the mental torture of Malcolm. For a few weeks she played mental games with him designed to undermine his curiosity and to let him know how greatly he disgusted her. The very sight of him released a rush of anger, and he became cowering and overly humble in her presence, smiling too frequently at her, up from under, his eyes fearful. This response only increased her anger.

"Don't pretend you like me," she would snap.

"I hate your smile," she would hiss.

"Just go away."

She only did this when they were alone together. She was sure no one knew the depths of her irritation. And at last, over breakfast, she said to John, "I think we ought to have a trial separation."

"What? Why?"

"I can't take another day of it."

"And what about the kids?"

She smiled, "I'll take Jessica, don't worry. You'll only have Malcolm to worry about."

"Oh no, wait a minute," he said, raising his hand like a traffic cop. "Uh-uh, no, that's the limit."

Carol nibbled bacon, looking down.

"Then what do you suggest?"

He smiled, "I'll take Jessica, and you take Malcolm."

"You've got to be kidding. Jessica would never stand for it. She'd want to be with me."

"Are you sure about that?"

He stood up at the sound of Malcolm calling loudly from his crib upstairs. It would turn to a cry in a minute, and John couldn't stand the sound of a crying child. Carol listened to him go, a soft patient pad up the stairs, and realized she was *not* sure about that. Jessica might want to be with her father, after all. It was a possibility she had neglected, and a pretty strong one.

"Oh God," she moaned, "maybe I'm stuck."

When John returned carrying Malcolm—who could walk—she looked at them and said, "Jessica wouldn't want to be parted from Malcolm. We better try to stick it out."

John said nothing. Like a young branch, he was a model of passive resistance. All he needed to be content was time and peace to pursue his mild activities. Carol realized he was not so much weak as pliable—one of the lucky ones who have no interest in power, glory, or mental games.

SPRING CAME, AND ROCKS were tossed against buses traveling around Boston. The newspapers and streets threw off images of small black faces pressed against glass, of cops and white teenagers and their mothers. The streets, warming up, were littered with debris and broken by potholes from snow plows. Whites didn't dare drive through black areas and blacks didn't dare drive through white areas. While great pink magnolias spread their wings along Commonwealth Avenue, yellow school buses folded and steamed only a few blocks away.

A couple of times Carol had to drive into perilous territory for a meeting, and for these occasions she brought Malcolm. Her black child would ward off danger, she believed. But at one meeting, a young black woman approached while Carol smilingly squeezed Malcolm on her lap. The woman ran her hands over Malcolm's ashy skin with a critical eye and said, "You don't know how to take care of him. His skin needs oil, it's dry."

Humiliated, Carol lied that she had just run out of oil and asked if the woman could recommend a special kind.

"Johnson's is just fine," said the woman.

Malcolm fussed through the hot meeting, so Carol took him home soon. She could not get up the energy to oil his limbs more than twice, and did not bring him to a meeting again. In the summer heat, his skin grew ashier still and developed scaly patches which he picked at. He was not a whiny child, but had outbursts of weeping from no apparent cause. Jessica was the only one who could handle these moods, and, like any older sister, cajoled him with false promises—candy, a trip, a game. The attention she gave him, inherent in even the falsest of promises, cheered him back into high spirits.

BY THE TIME HE WAS THREE, the scabs on Malcolm's skin were an embarrassment to Carol, and she took him to the neighborhood clinic. The doctor said it was a form of eczema and recommended a special cream. Dutifully, Carol got John or Jessica to apply the cream to Malcolm's dry spots, but they didn't clear.

With the arrival of June, the prospect of sweltering out a whole summer in the city was intolerable. So the family splurged on a beach house for two weeks, and were, for the first time in years, free from the obsessions of urban living. A private beach, an acre of land on Cape Cod, and they were happy. It seemed to Carol, then, that they were suffering unduly by their life in the city.

"Maybe we should think of moving," she said to John from the screen porch; they could hear, through the darkness, the sea lapping over rocks.

"I've been thinking the same thing," he said.

"But your job."

"I'm never going to get tenure, so why stick around? I could probably earn as much money as a carpenter."

"But where should we go?"

"California?"

"I'd be near my mother again," she said with great joy.

THEIR RETURN TO THE CITY'S HEAT only increased their determination to leave. They had the capital to move without difficulty, and John sent in a letter of resignation to the college on the first of August. Carol put the house on the market for a sale sometime in the fall. They hoped to leave around Christmas.

Malcolm was sent to an overcrowded day care, for full days, as soon as he was toilet trained. Carol chose to send him to one of the more understaffed and ill-equipped day cares because of the predominance of black children there. She felt, she said, he needed as much contact with his own race as he could get. She also felt, but did not say, that he was society's responsibility because he was not quite her own. Besides, she had to devote herself to the problems of moving, and had to drive Jessica from lesson to lesson and friend to friend, which was exhausting.

At the day care, Malcolm was either ingratiating or sobbing. He gazed up the length of grownups with the eyes of a beggar. Often he sat by himself picking at his scabs, and once when the head teacher asked him to stop, he said he was "just picking the paint off."

"What paint?" she asked.

"That. Black paint." He pointed at his skin.

The head teacher promptly reported this remark to Carol, who cried, "He said *that?*"

After weeks of avoiding it, she noticed Malcolm again. This time she placed his image in the future against a flat blue California sky, palm trees, and oranges. The Pacific Coast, as she knew it, meant the life of the body, the health behind the smile—all golden, tow-headed, blond. Malcolm, small, black, and covered with sores like some Indian beggar, did not exactly fit.

"Will there be other blacks in La Jolla?" John asked her, out of the blue.

"I know a couple with an adopted daughter; she's mixed, but I think they're still there."

"Maybe we should go to L.A. or San Diego."

"That's not the point of our moving!"

"True," he agreed.

Another day, dropping Malcolm at day care, she saw a handsome black couple taking leave of two daughters at the door, and she said to Malcolm, "Wouldn't you like to have parents like that? They look just like you."

He smiled and nodded, uneasily.

SOMETIMES A CHILD IS BORN—or bought—into a family in which it never feels comfortable. It is almost as if he or she has been sent as a messenger on an errand that has gone astray and is held prisoner by these strangers for many years. Yet it never occurs to anyone involved that there may have been some mistake made, at the level of supernatural cause, to produce this situation. And so the child suffers, as do the parents.

One of the ways they all survive is by the presence of a sister or brother. For a while, the mutual interests of childhood bind the children together, and even if there is fighting, there is communication. For the messenger child, who is being held prisoner, this sister becomes the object around which he or she grows. All strengths and weaknesses, later ascribed to the acts of the mother and father, are actually constituted through the sibling.

For Malcolm, whose presence in the family was openly insecure, Jessica was the source of his development and happiness. From her, he learned what was acceptable, what was laughable, what was wrong. His fear at finding himself in an overcrowded day care was not that he was far from home, but that Jessica was not with him, guiding and protecting him. He was surrounded by boisterous aliens. Because of his timidity, he was left on the sidelines, forgotten but observant.

What was he doing there? Where would they put him next? Who would tell him when to move? Who would unzip his pants if he had to pee? When was he going to leave? His mind was awash with unanswered questions. He only knew that if he smiled at a grownup, he would be left alone, and could play with some toy in peace. While playing, he would hum one of the songs Jessica had taught him, and feel her presence hovering over his head.

The house was filling up with cardboard boxes. The days were growing chill, the leaves falling. Malcolm got a bad chest cold and had to stay home for a few days. With Jessica in school, he tried to stay out of Carol's way, upstairs in his bedroom, playing and coughing.

She wanted to be pleased with his behavior, but instead his humility annoyed her, his meek smile became to her like a spray of poison. His eyes expected the worst from her, and brought it out. She teased him mercilessly. She had never, since childhood, indulged herself in cruelty for its own sake the way children can do, turning against the weakest one available for sport. With a limpid curiosity, she knew what she was doing, clearly, and did it more.

15

"You hate me, don't you," she said. "After all I've done for you, you hate me. I can't believe it. Don't pretend you like me, with that smile, you don't have to smile, you can just come out and say it, you hate me. I'm not even your real mother, so why pretend."

Malcolm stared at the baloney sandwich in his hand.

"I know Jessica told you everything, more than once. She's mine, out of my body, but you're not. So you can go ahead and hate me."

He laid down his sandwich and concentrated on picking at a scab on his left wrist.

"Don't do that!" she cried, slapping at his hand. "You're making it worse. Eat."

"I'm not hungry," he murmured.

"I asked you if you wanted a sandwich and you said yes. Now eat it."

She hung over him, from behind, feeling herself capable of physical violence as she never had before. He started to pick up the sandwich, but she grabbed it from him and crushed it in her hand, throwing it across the kitchen into the sink.

"Go upstairs," she said.

He did so, immediately. Sitting in his chair, Carol felt a gush of compassion and guilt. But she stayed still, as if it were enough to feel it, for, sure enough, all feelings pass.

"This can't go on," she said, and sobbed.

Now she thought of the people she knew, in the city, the neighborhood, how they had been watching her for symptoms of failure since the day she brought Malcolm home. She had, she thought, successfully concealed all signs of trouble from the public eye. But Malcolm's eczema, the quality of his skin, was giving her away. Many commented on it, eyeing her. What a relief that she was leaving!

But then she recalled some changes in Jessica's behavior. Her daughter was conscious of her mother's attitudes, and was becoming overtly protective, at home, of Malcolm. She would defend her little brother for the smallest infraction of the rules, and say to her mother, "Don't be mean to him," or, "I did it, not him."

And this was more than Carol could bear. The loss of her daughter's respectful adoration was bound to happen some day, when she was a teenager maybe, but not now. And, given the fact that they were all moving west together, there was no escape from the problem. She refused to go on feeling she was a prisoner in her own house, the victim of this child.

"Why, I wonder, do I feel this way about him?" she asked herself. And this was the one question she never asked anyone else, then or later, when it became necessary.

SNOW CAME, A LEVEL FILM of white, a hint of the deeper end of winter. Wonderful, then, to imagine golden bulbs of fruit, and not electric lighting, as the gift of a season. Boxes were already heading west; the furniture would leave the morning of the day they left in their car. Two weeks before their departure, as the snow fell, Jessica said to her mother from her pillow and bed, "Will Malcolm and me share a room in California?"

"I don't know," said Carol.

She sank to the edge of her daughter's bed, and could see from there the white drops floating and dissolving against the glass.

"Why?" she asked Jessica.

"I just wondered."

"I honestly don't know," she said, "if he's coming or not, with us."

"What?"

"I mean, I don't know."

"Come on, Mom," the girl sat up, "what happened? Did his real mother find him? Does she want him back?"

Carol closed her eyes behind her glasses. "Yes," she said, "exactly. How did you guess? But don't tell him!"

"I won't, I promise—but did you see her, what does she look like?"

"I didn't see her, they won't let me. You know. But I think he'd be happier with her, don't you?"

Jessica said she guessed so, and her mother stood up, drifting toward the door.

"Now go to sleep," she called. She didn't turn back, for she had confidence in her daughter, that she would sleep on command, almost, or at least be quiet until she fell asleep.

Jessica had, unwittingly, given her mother directions to the exit she had been seeking.

Carol went downstairs and sat in the living room with a pile of sewing. John was playing some Bach pieces on the harpsichord. Malcolm had been asleep since seven. Carol, biting a loose button off a pair of Malcolm's pajamas, wore the expression of one watching an intense battle scene on television. It was being played out on John's thin back, hunched over the keys.

"IT'S THE BEST TIME TO DO IT," she told him. "Now. While we're leaving."

"So your friends won't know?"

"Well, that's part of it, I admit. But for Jessica, too. If we return him to the state now, it will just be part of the whole separation from the East Coast."

"She'll still feel it. Deeply."

"Not if she thinks he's going to his real mother. That will seem like justice. You know how children like justice."

John squirmed, "But what about him?"

"He'll be better off. They'll find a nice black family for him. He'll be miserable in California, he'll feel like a freak. And you know it hasn't been working out—look at his skin, it just hasn't worked."

"I didn't think it was that bad," said John.

"Well, you're in a dream world."

He gazed off into space with a rueful air. For she was not altogether wrong in this judgment. While he considered himself a good and honorable man, most of his life was acted out in his head, which made certain portions of it readily disposable. He did not have an addictive or dependent personality. Wherever he went, he would feel the same things, behave the same way. This abstract manner of surviving made him easy to live with. Like Carol, his one visceral passion was his daughter. He loved Malcolm no more or less than the sheepdog, Mozart. He did not exactly imagine that Malcolm had the same emotions that he did, though if someone suggested he dehumanized Malcolm, he would eagerly protest.

"I honestly don't think it's right," he said to Carol.

"I wanted a mixed female," said Carol. "Besides, I had no conception of the problems it involved."

"You meant well."

"Right."

"Hmmm," he sighed.

He looked at his wife with faint disapproval, but thought "peace at any cost."

"It's the best thing," she said.

Moral righteousness, being an essential tool for survival, entered both of their hearts. He felt morally superior to her; she felt morally justified to the state.

BUT THE SOCIAL WORKER did not see it this way. She was mad.

"You realize he'll be passed from foster home to foster home from now on," she lectured. "He's too old to be adopted, except by some miracle, and he'll probably end up in the streets. People do return babies, it's true—it's not unusual for a white couple to return a black or mixed child. But always within the first few months. You've had this child for nearly three years! How could you wait so long?"

"I was trying my hardest," said Carol, "to make it work."

"And you failed."

Carol's eyes burned. The question of failure had not risen in her mind before. Not of her failure, anyway.

"It's not that simple," she said.

"You are making it that simple, just by this act—by returning him to the state like a pair of shoes that don't fit."

"I'm sorry—"

"Forget it," snapped the fat white woman. "Bring him in on Monday morning."

"But the movers are coming then."

The woman gave Carol a look of such intense intolerance that Carol blushed and jumped up.

"Okay," she swore, "I'll bring him in."

THE ICY AIR OUTDOORS made her teeth cold; she was grinding them unconsciously, feeling sore inside and out. "Things do work out for the best, you must have faith," a priest once told her, "though it may not be the best for you, but for someone else."

"What a horrible thought."

Still, she was consoled at home by Jessica's romantic faith that Malcolm was going to be reunited with his mother. Carol almost came to believe it herself as she listened to Jessica imagine the first meeting between mother and son.

"Can't I tell him?" she begged Carol.

"No, dear. The social worker said to let it be a surprise."

"But why?"

"I don't know. They have all these ideas, fascists."

"You don't like them?"

"They are interfering, to put it mildly."

"I wish I could see what she looks like! Do you think

she'll look like Malcolm? It'll be *weird*. Can't I come too, when you bring him?"

"No, dear."

JESSICA HAD A HARD TIME keeping the news from Malcolm. It was almost more than she could bear, and the repression of her instinct worked havoc on her stomach. She couldn't eat, and developed an intense belly ache. She lay flat, face down, on Malcolm's bed while he played with his trucks. His suitcase was already half-packed through meticulous folding, the way Carol always worked. As Jessica eyed its open mouth, her innards tightened, she wanted to cry.

Malcolm asked, "Tummy ache?"

"Yes," she moaned.

"Want to throw up?"

"Yes. But I can't. Nothing will come up."

"Oh."

He lowered his chin and growled for his truck's engine, sliding it across the bare floor; the shag rug was already rolled and ready to go. Jessica watched him, noting that his manipulation of the truck was more sophisticated than it was a week before, his growl more true to life.

"Make it crash," she instructed him.

He whirled it up against the wall, roaring and wailing as it knocked gently against his suitcase.

"Pretty good," she said. "You're getting good at trucks."

"I am?"

"Yup. Come on, let's have a race."

She slid off the bed and joined him on the floor, for a short time forgetting the mysterious forces at work on the two of them.

BUT INEVITABLY MALCOLM LEFT the next morning. John and Jessica cried when he was gone. Rain fell in mushy, half-frozen lumps against the window. Carol was taking it upon herself to bring him downtown. Gray snow was piled in dense heaps along the edges of the streets. Traffic ground slowly forward, windshield wipers bopping.

Carol appraised Malcolm's wide-eyed stare. He knew that he was not going to "California," but somewhere else. That was all he knew. Carol thought of all the boring papers she would have to sign—it would probably take all morning—and considered changing her mind. The hostility of the social workers was almost more than she could bear, and she sighed.

"How do you feel?"

He shrugged from inside his blue snowsuit.

"Well, everything will be alright. Don't worry."

He was quiet then murmured, "Mommy?"

"What," curtly.

"Are you going to pick me up?"

"Uh, you have to spend the night there."

She reached out and turned on the radio. The morning news surfaced with the usual tales of urban disaster—fires, robbery, mugging, murder, rape—to which she listened, proudly, because she would be free of it all soon.

When they finally parked, she looked at the gray building and considered going home again. They got out and

Malcolm slipped on the ice, so she had to hold both his hand and his bag. The pressure of his hand raised a vague emotional quarrel, but she was a reasonable person, and her reasons came to mind, fast, not the least of them being that he would be better off without her. They crossed the street, gingerly.

On the other side, they went through the red doors together; and, some time later, she came out, alone.

FIDELITY

PAUL RANG THE DOORBELL as his train roared through his head and west to Forest Hills. The dawn was wet and gold on the girders supporting the El. Or the Hell, as he called it. Noise and squalor huddled together in the same part of his mind that waited for her to answer the door and let him in. He felt the usual fear, a kind of cringing snarl in his stomach, at the approach of her rage. His clothes were creased and his face, hung over.

This time Mary walked casually down the dark hallway in her bleached nightgown after letting him in. Her footsteps were light. The hall smelled of baby—not vomit, but sweet clothes and powder, which he inhaled as if it were merciful incense.

He didn't follow her or apologize, but started stripping, tripping, as he veered towards the kitchen. Shoes, socks, trousers, shirt. He dropped all but the shoes in the plastic laundry basket and picked up Yeats' *Collected Poems* off the kitchen table. Took them to the bathroom to read.

The trees are in their autumn beauty,
The woodland paths are dry,
Under the October twilight the water
Mirrors a still sky;
Upon the brimming water among the stones
Are nine-and-fifty swans.

Doors away the children were rising from sleep. She heard them from her bed, the baby damp under her arm;

27

she gathered him close, although she ached, comfortably. As usual she imagined some evil finding one of the children, and her structure, the system of her time, being wrecked forever. Often she lay in the dark or light imagining pitfalls, deep waters, insidious disease, swallowing up the children. Her heartbeat would speed; she would pray, knock wood, make vows, to ward off the possibility of loss. It seemed to her a form of insanity, to worry so, and she never talked about it to anyone. Now she heard the padding footsteps coming; they would join her in bed, half asleep, warm and damp.

He flushed the toilet and headed for a cool shower. Little good it would do. Suds around his chest, underarms, neck and ears. Like washing the outside of a dish and leaving the inside scummy. Sleep was the only wash for the inside, and he doubted if he'd get that. The bed would be full of her anger and their children. Or maybe this time there would be only sulking and coldness; the anger had been tapering off lately, and he couldn't think why.

She watched him enter with the towel around his waist, his bony limbs moist and pale. Automatically, she turned around the children, as if he were a cloud passing over the sun.

"I'm tired. Move over, kids."

"We're getting up anyway," she said.

"It's only seven."

"I can't sleep anymore."

"What are you going to do?"

"What do you think?"

"I can't think."

"Then sleep."

She took the baby with her and the other children followed, chattering. They went down the stairs, discussing orange juice and cereal and spoons of sugar. She was thinking of her aunt, who had nine children, and when one of them was killed, she said it didn't matter how many you had, the way people thought it did, the loss of one was the end of happiness, for good.

She wondered if Paul had these anxieties. He was loving with the children and treated them as he did everyone else. Recklessly, with charm. He didn't give much or get much back, as if there weren't anything he wanted, really. That's what it came down to. What you wanted, and how badly. The trains rumbled above the windows, shaking them, every few minutes. She hardly noticed it any more, except in brief flashes of fear. The kitchen was dark but tidy. She turned on a light and began the rituals, laying out bowls and spoons for four, and her coffee cup. She put the baby in his pram beside the stove and snapped at the others to be quiet. She noticed her copy of Yeats was missing. Cursed.

He heard her, and made a grimace. Every noise—the slam of the ice box, the clink of a dish—zoomed down the hall like a bullet at him. She had a right to be angry, but he preferred a direct shout. He waited, and now that she was quiet, he imagined her sulkily drinking her coffee, and for a moment he closed his eyes, vaguely bereaved by her silence.

She had not found Yeats anywhere, and so instead read Matthew Arnold's "The Forsaken Merman," trying to decide if it was too old for the children.

Come, dear children, let us away;
Down and away below.
Now my brothers call from the bay;
Now the great winds shorewards blow;
Now the salt tides seawards flow;
Now the wild white horses play,
Champ and chafe and toss in the spray.
Children, dear, let us away.
This way, this way . . .

She loved it, pushed away her coffee and watched the children eat, soothed by the sight of appetites in progress. All grownups, she noticed, hung around children eating—not only to pick at the remains of the food, but to get some comfort.

Her silence began to needle him, and he put on a pair of pants and went down the thin hall, barefoot.

"Go play somewhere," he said to the children. "You're finished. Give your mother a break."

They dispersed, obediently, to the living room, a drab room sunk in a clutter of toys and crayons, where they watched TV. Mary sat with the baby on her lap, kissing its neck.

"I thought you were sleeping," she said.

"How could I with all that noise? You shouting."

"You didn't need to come home."

"You wish I hadn't?"

"It doesn't matter."

"You want me to move out?"

She shrugged. They stared at each other's eyes.

"I hate scenes. You know that."

He poured himself some coffee, lit a cigarette and sat down away from her.

"You hate scenes?" he said. "Ha. I remember a few, not so long ago, you enjoyed."

"Enjoyed?"

"I'm sorry," he said, "really. I was stupid. Smoked and drank and passed out."

"Yeah? Where?"

"At Bobbie's. Call him if you don't believe me."

"I won't bother."

"Why not?"

She got up and went to the refrigerator. The backs of her legs were marked by blue veins; he was glad he couldn't see them. They came with the second baby and never left. He never mentioned them to her, and didn't know if she knew they were there. He thought of the muscular legs of a girl he had slept with recently and tried to justify the comparison. But nothing happened. There was no comparison. His wife was like his mother in his mind, outside the normal fields and runnings. And the desire to leave home always ended this way, in physical details which filled him with pity for her.

"Why won't you call Bobbie?" he said belligerently.

She didn't answer, and he noticed she was making a concoction of egg, whipped cream, sugar, and a spot of bourbon—one-handedly, the baby on her hip. It was a hangover drink they had together a couple of times. He got up and took the baby from her.

"What's that?" he asked, as if he didn't know.

"For your head. We're out of aspirin."

An emotion like nostalgia passed through his limbs. He felt like crying. For her. For himself. He didn't know for whom. He put his head on the baby's.

"You've got to work tonight," she said, "so you better get some sleep."

"I should be a patient, not an orderly."

"Really," she agreed.

"No, I'll take the kids out this morning so you can rest."

"I don't need a rest."

"You went to bed early?"

"Nine. The usual."

He wanted to raise the subject of his night out again, if only to apologize, or make her mad. But she wasn't interested. She handed him a glass, instead, of golden frothy eggnog, and took the baby back for herself. He took the glass out to the living room and told the kids to get dressed. Opening the front door, he saw the sun was no longer golden, but flat, and the sidewalks glittered with tin and litter.

His depression did not pass out of him, even as he sipped at the drink. He felt he had a soft center, like bad fruit, and it was sinking under the thumbs of the sun. He shut the door and watched her pass by him with the baby, each cooing over the other's flesh. Her belly, which had been large and stiff so recently, was a contrast to his own soft center. She had told him about the baby sliding out, umbilicus flashing turquoise in the glare of the delivery room lights. He had missed it all, each time, out of fear. No more chances, he was sure.

Now she called to him to help the children dress, and her voice was austere and maternal. He moved, obediently, in that direction, heavily conscious that she didn't care about the night before. He wasn't on her mind that way at all! This freedom was all that he had ever desired, to be able to come and go without suffering her resentment at the end. But now that he had what he wanted, it was horrible to discover that she did too.

RADICAL LOVE

NEAR THE END of the Cold War, I lived in Boston. It was not where I wanted to be. In those days it was a drab and chaotic city, segregated by race, ethnicity, and class, with poorly educated and self-serving community leaders who invariably mishandled the funding they were given. Nothing improved from year to year. Naturally I took any escape I could get whenever it was offered. Otherwise I felt I was dissolving into the ashen light of the office where I worked as a community organizer.

One winter night I went to a dinner party—eagerly, I have to say—given by some philanthropic folk I had known for years on Beacon Hill. I felt quite shy and hung near the jungle of potted plants that embraced a window which was heavily curtained and dark. I knew exactly what the social components were, or thought I did. This was not the moneyed sector—Republican—but an aristocracy of letters and public service—Democrat. Edwardian furniture, collectors' books and prints, chandeliers frayed or dusty, and the vast assortment of plants—these created an environment as natural as a city garden partially gone to seed. There were about as many people present as there were chairs, in professions either artistic or academic.

We had roast beef with all the trimmings—Yorkshire pudding, gravy, potatoes, brussel sprouts—and a snow pudding for dessert. During the meal I was struck by a man sitting opposite me, who suddenly blurted out a quote from Chekhov. He said, "Everything that has been written about love is not a solution, but only a statement of questions that have remained unanswered."

There was a pause in the clink and chatter around me; I noticed the whiteness of the faces converting into shadows as they all turned away from him simultaneously. He hadn't glanced at me even once until then, but now when I proudly murmured the word "Chekhov," he began quoting more and more lines about love, addressing them to me. If I identified the origin of a line, he raised his glass to me in an annoyingly patronizing way.

After dinner and over brandy, I found myself beside the same man. He was, as it turned out, an English professor, around forty years old. He was an incongruous combination of preppie and practical, and I wondered if he had ties to the CIA. He smoked in great heaves, and flashed fabulous smiles at inappropriate moments. Very good-looking in a sandy WASP way. When I told him I was involved in social work, though he certainly hadn't asked, he became excited. He was eager, he said, to understand an event in his life, and wondered if I could help him.

"Years ago, when I was at Harvard—it was the late fifties—I adopted an academic family. They were very much the same as these people here tonight—gentle liberals, you might say. My background was East Side–Wall Street, New York. The Lewis family was everything my own family was not—literary and intellectual. I was fascinated. They asked me to cocktails and Sunday lunches in their rather shabby house on the edge of the lower-class section of Cambridge. They had a son and a daughter. The son,

Jamie, was quite wild. He rushed around Harvard Square in a Lenin-like beard and cap with a dirty red star sewed onto his pea jacket. His parents worried over his drinking, not his ideas, and set me up as a model of restraint.

"Their daughter, Emily, was thirteen when I met her. A freckle-faced tomboy. She was usually lying on her stomach on the hall stairs, in faded dungarees and sneakers, reading comics or Chinese poetry. She was a comforting figure to me, in my anxiety to please, because it was clear from the outset that she had a crush on me. I had no sisters. I was nineteen. She was the ideal *copain*, as they say in France, for me.

"I took her to movies and plays and coffee houses, helped her with her homework, and recommended books. Of course, I had girlfriends at college, was almost always in love with someone, and I told Emily all about them. She was both precocious and innocent. She gave me advice, based on facts like thin lips, weak chins and make-up, which I volunteered in my descriptions. Or she'd say things like, 'I guess low bottoms on short legs are sexy, but you can't walk behind her all the time.'

"In those days, as you probably know yourself, we didn't have sex. That is, not the whole thing. We were, on the other hand, connoisseurs in the art of necking. Those were the days. The horrible truth of the matter is that promiscuity has ruined sex.

"In any case, all my descriptions of passion were clean, pure, romantic. And Emily made the perfect listener for someone who considered himself both questing and jaded. I luxuriated in her idealization of me, and threw out the occasional come-on with an affectionate name or embrace. I imagined that her passion for dogs and poetry was equal to her passion for me!

"I had no reason to believe otherwise. She went into adolescence in a completely normal way. She hung out, after school, with her friends in Harvard Square. They would sneak cigarettes, look at boys, discuss weight and hair. All that. She was sort of reddish-gold in her appearance. That coloring always seemed to me to emanate from and perfectly express her fiery inner life. Because she did, always, have something fiery and reckless about her, which made me a little nervous. It also attracted me, on occasion.

"Now, to this day I can't see that what I did was wrong, or misleading. I mean, at the time it seemed like an act of love and acknowledgment of her particular beauty. I took her out one night in my last spring at college—to a movie—then walked her home. Her delirious happiness was infectious, like the heavy scent of lilacs draping our path, and I thought, Oh what the hell. I love her! And I told her that, and how I would, one day, marry her. When? she asked. After all my sins are exhausted, I told her.

"Then, with her face afire with joy, she looked up at me hopefully, and I responded as she wanted me to. We necked under the lilac trees, in someone's garden, and she would—let's face it—have gone all the way, as they say, except for my self-control. After all I hadn't forgotten how young she was, or that I would be leaving shortly.

"Afterwards she insisted that I reassure her of my intention to marry her when I was perhaps thirty, and I took her home. She was like a walking ode to joy. At the time I think I believed, myself, that we would marry years and years from then. It was a sort of pact based on hope—for the future, for its predictability, for the endurance of emotions."

At this point, I thought the story was over and began to scramble for my bag; but he patted my wrist quickly and went on talking.

"Well, soon after, I graduated and went off into the world. A band of us from Harvard drifted around Paris, Rome, and Morocco. We imagined we were writers in exile ... from what? Who knows? We all had enough money to squander, and access to respectable jobs at home, whenever we chose. Emily was not so lucky. Her family never had any money. So the only way she could follow me was by mail. Which she did, almost everywhere I went. It was alarming in one way, and vaguely reassuring in another. The American Express, in every city I visited, contained a letter to me from Emily. I rarely answered her.

"When I finally wound up in New York, she began to visit me. I was always amused by her. But occasionally I was put off by her tense approach and the question in her eyes. She seemed to work a kind of alchemy on my character, so that vices were turned into virtues. I felt I lived a second existence in her mind. The way you feel, say, when someone relatively unknown announces that they have dreamed about you. I tried to tell her how low I was, what a failure, but she wouldn't listen, laugh and say something like, You're just a late bloomer. It means you'll live a long time.

"She went to college in Canada, in her typically peculiar fashion. Anyone else from her background would have gone to Radcliffe or Wellesley. But not Emily. Montreal was exotic. Also, I suspect that she got a good deal, economically, there. Her parents could hardly afford much. Christmas and summers she returned home, and always sought me out.

"For my part, various attempts at writing and publishing had turned into failures. And I returned, somewhat sheepishly, to the security of academia. Harvard took me in; I lingered over the PhD atrocity for four years. And then I began teaching what Professor Lewis had taught—English Literature. Living in Cambridge, it was easy for Emily to visit me.

"But in one of her longer absences, I got married. To a woman named Emma—Cambridge girl, like Emily, but younger, prettier, and much, much richer. She was tame, familiar, and neurasthenic. Our love lit up when the lights went off, so to speak.

"I was surprised, one summer day, by a visit, at my office, from Emily. She was very high-spirited, excited by her work in public television and her life, and I asked her to come to dinner that very night so that I could hear all about it. I half-assumed she knew I was married, but part of me was unable to say it. I didn't want to disappoint her, I suppose, and took the coward's way.

"The result was disastrous, as the results of cowardice always are. When she arrived, dressed to the nines, my wife let her in. From behind, I introduced them. I saw Emily's color change, as a sudden light changes on a windowpane. She seemed to become invisible in substance. Violence tends to come in this form—like a shadow, an atmosphere, not as a body. She slammed her purse against poor Emma, and said in a five-year-old's voice: 'A wife?

You're his wife? I don't believe it! What a laugh! He can't have a wife. It's a joke, a fraud, and I'll get you for it. You'll see. I'll get you. I'll put a curse on you! Let this house stink with misery from now on. Let everything in it rot and die. Let there be no children, no happiness, never!' And she slammed Emma with the purse again, and disappeared.

"You must think I'm inventing this. It's very hard to describe credibly. I mean, it's the kind of violence you would only expect to come from a completely different class. Both Emma and I were literally destroyed by it. The whole atmosphere of our house was transformed as if by a can of spray, a wand—by magic! Plants died. Food burned. There was no child, for no reason. Emma became increasingly idle. Lay about like an invalid, unable to go out on the streets. Wan and sleepy, or mad with anxiety, she blamed her afflictions on me. She went home to her parents, finally, and that was the end of that.

"I had two reactions. I worked harder than ever, moving up the academic ranks. And I had a series of indiscriminate affairs. A couple of times I had vivid dreams about Emily. Terribly sad ones, if you know the kind. She seemed to have crossed some Stygian boundary and entered my unconscious, drenched with grief. There was, too, something seductive about her in these dreams.

"Finally, as I knew she would, she wrote me a lengthy letter, apologizing for her behavior and announcing her impending marriage to a Canadian; it closed with a series of questions about my wife's welfare and happiness. She was in Toronto then. The distance seemed safe.

"So I wrote back and told her of the end of my marriage. I also mentioned how hard to was for me to imagine her married to anyone at all! Within a month, Emily was back in my office, saying she couldn't live in Canada any more, it was not as lively as America, and she had discovered that she was not in love—in a deep way—with the Canadian. She had a job in Boston.

"My feelings were mixed, to say the least. I still loved to talk to her. She was so familiar, it was almost like being alone, in a conversation with oneself. But she seemed dangerous now, unpredictable, and definitely unsexy. To me anyway. I could, at that time, understand why other men might find her desirable—and she certainly had no shortage of admirers and affairs—but for me her very presence signified a kind of termination to life; the end. By her extraordinary persistence and constancy, Emily seemed to defy a basic law of nature, the law that keeps things moving, shifting.

"During that time, I saw her a couple of times, and always kept it public, safe. I was lonely, though, and finally wanted to try marriage again. I longed for it until I married the first logical woman to cross my path. Alice—a successful public relations woman. We both wanted children, soon, in the desperate way of aging couples in fairy tales.

"Our wish was granted. And we did all the things you do to celebrate—bought a house, furniture, a part-time housekeeper. I felt secure, and happy again, waiting for our child. My daughter, Eva. That little baby brought me more happiness than I ever imagined. It was as if I hadn't known I existed, in the flesh, before I had a child. I could see why people had dozens of children, recklessly. I worried over her night and day."

Now I interrupted him with felicitations and again tried to leave the chair for the door, but he waved his hand in the air to stop me. I fell back. He went on.

"When Emily reappeared, as she was bound to do, I was reluctant to see her. But right off she told me she had heard I was now a father. She was full of seemingly sincere congratulations, so I relaxed and met her in a loud boothy place where we had a prolonged lunch, talking intimately. She kept insisting that she hoped I stayed married, this time, whether I was happy or not.

"I took this to mean that she felt better herself with me out of the way. It freed her. I even teased her about that and she teased me about being the one who finds it hard to keep his promises. There was a sadness running under all our jokes, as I see it now. It seemed to me to be the end of a future between us. I don't know why it bothered me then, but it did.

"That night, when I got home, the baby was ill. A raging fever. It turned out to be meningitis, and she barely survived. Alice and I hung over her night and day. And when we knew that Eva was going to be all right, Alice said she couldn't take it. She wanted out. I thought she was just exhausted by the horror of the experience. But no, she was serious. She wanted me to keep the baby, to raise her. It was not her cup of tea, as she put it, to be eaten alive by a child.

"There is, as you know, a limit to the sudden changes a person can suffer, especially as he or she approaches forty. I reached that limit. I had to take a leave of absence from work. Nearly cracked up completely. It was only the

45

necessity of caring for the baby that kept me going. And I organized myself around that.

"I couldn't look at other women, but huddled away, drinking too much, in my over-sized house. One day a pair of Jehovah's Witnesses came to the door. One of them was a double for Emily. And after I took the little booklet proclaiming the end of the world, and sent them away, I began to assess my personal history, seeing Emily as the one constant in it.

"In a rush, I called her. It didn't surprise me when she answered, or when she agreed, immediately, to see me. The whole point of Emily was her consistency, and I knew she had a studio apartment in Cambridgeport, regular work as a journalist, friends, the usual set of circumstances for someone of her age and class.

"We met a couple of days later. I remember that the trees were covered with glassy drippings, frozen rain-drops that gleamed furiously in the sun. Branches rattled and showered particles of ice. It was a Sunday, and I wait-ed for her inside the door of the same boothy restaurant where we usually met. I was quite excited, and looked for-ward to seeing her face light up when I told her our time had, at last, arrived.

"The fairyland aspect of the day I'll never forget. It was like life *inside* a mirror. And Emily arrived, rosy-cheeked and smiling, an image of health within this silvery frame. I thrilled at the sight of her, and sat across from her at the table, thinking how it was only the first of endless tables across which we would meet. She chatted about me and the baby as generously as before. I realized it was always this way. She talked and asked about me, let me go on for hours, and only told me the essentials about herself—very quickly. I told her all about my daughter, suggesting her need for a real mother and my need for a wife who would never leave me.

"She became quieter then, and I imagined her sensing the direction I was taking. I wanted to draw it out, enjoy the suspension. After all, years had passed between us! But then she said she had something to thank me for. I asked what, curious. For never loving me, she replied. The solemnity—and the contentment—hidden in these words made me lean back, take a breath. I couldn't immediately react. She went on, saying, 'I learned how to love God, and that's all I every really wanted to learn.'

"I laughed, of course. I thought my little friend—once a socialist, then an anarchist, then an atheist, and always a rebel—must be joking. But no, she was serious that she was actually converting to Catholicism, with the intention of entering an order. And she insisted that the unrequited nature of her love for me had served as a kind of instruction. I was staggered. I couldn't take it all in. Couldn't even speak.

"She was without pretension or silliness of any kind. Her conversion was clearly profound and obliterating to all other attachments. I felt like an oaf, sitting there with my expectations and hopes for us. And finally I was able to speak to her—out of some anger, I must admit, and hurt pride. And I told her what I had planned to say: We should get married; I was ready. I wanted and needed her. I said it all fast, from the heart, but watched closely to see her reaction. Part of me knew it was a test—for her, perhaps the final test of this love or faith she was professing.

47

"What do you think?" he asked me, but didn't listen or wait for an answer. I watched the room around us beginning to empty.

"This was three years ago, you understand, but I can see and feel it all as if it were yesterday. She looked at me, dumbfounded, her eyes slowly filling with tears. She shook her head from side to side, slightly and slowly, as if I had just disappointed her by offering her everything she had ever wanted. I felt a rush of shame—it literally made me blush—as I saw her reach for her coat, get ready to go, her expression dull and weary.

"She stood up, then, pausing beside me to say good-bye. For good, she added enigmatically. I reached out to take her hand, to touch her, but she slipped away and was gone before I could utter any more of the feelings in me . . . And that was it. I haven't seen her again. I won't. It's awful. What do you say to such a story? Can you tell me?"

His face leaned in, boyish in its questioning. Most of the people were going, or had gone. I said something about patience and desire being the possessions of religious love, not sexual or romantic, and so I could see what Emily meant by thanking him. I told him that I, of all people, should know what she meant. And I added that his proposal, at the time, must have been very painful to her.

He tossed back his hair, got to his feet, and said, "I suppose uncertainty is one way of keeping young."

I followed him to the door to say goodnight to our hostess. She drew me back towards the closet, hurriedly, a shrewd woman in late middle age.

"Did he bore you with that Emily story of his? It's an obsession."

"I wasn't bored."

"I think he's lived too long in the sanctuary of literature. After all, everyone has disappointments in love," she said, "because love itself is disappointing."

"I don't think Emily found it disappointing," I said too quickly for her to bother responding. When I turned to leave, the English professor was waiting for me. He walked me to my car, a man of manners in a dated sort of way, and completely self-absorbed. I suspected he had not even heard my response to his story—but then, with a charm which must have riveted Emily, he smiled and revealed that he had heard some of it.

"It might, as you say, have been a religious passion all along," he said, "but I'm still not convinced, I'm still unsettled."

"Then what do you think it means?" I asked him.

"Too late is all it means. Those two terrible words—too late. And they are far from an answer."

Then he thanked me for listening and waited until I was locked in my car. We waved goodbye and I drove back into the darker, dingier part of town. I wondered why he didn't realize—as a connoisseur of Chekhov—that the meaning of a story is found in the middle, not in the end.

THE BLUE POOL

IT SEEMED TO Marcia Norris that the autumn had arrived while she was in the hospital. The month was still August, and she had only been in the ward two days. But when she went in, the heat was bright green; and when she came out, it had an orange tint to it. She lay on a lounge chair in her back yard, watching, suspiciously, the leaves that lay—one, two, three—under her crab-apple tree. Even the blue pool held evidence of fall. The net was spotted with leaves dragged off the surface of the water.

She had taken the phone out onto the patio, so it was within arm's reach when it rang. She had expected to hear the inquiring voice of her husband, Dan, or any one of her concerned neighborhood friends. Instead, it was a surprise.

"Kitty!" Marcia screeched at the voice of her old child-hood friend. "Where *are* you? I've *got* to see you!"

"Here. In Boston."

"Alone? With the children? What?"

"Just with Andrew," was the reply. Kitty's voice, always soft and a little husky, was both of these to an extreme.

"He's the youngest—right?" Marcia's eyes, behind her dark glasses, were wide and focused.

"Right. He's seven."

"Well, bring him along! Come on out."

"I don't have a car."

"Damn," said Marcia, "that's awful. Because I can hardly move. I just got out of the hospital."

"Oh, no. What for?"

"I'll tell you when you get here. But let me think." Marcia squeezed her kneecap and screwed her mouth to chew the inside of her lip. "There's a trolley," she said, after a pause. "You can get it in Copley Square, I think. Ask. It'll take you right to Chestnut Hill. I can somehow get over there to meet you. Okay?"

"Okay," said Kitty, "Is any time alright?"

"Don't be ridiculous. Of course! Hurry though. I can't wait to tell you everything."

AN HOUR LATER MARCIA GOT THE CALL from a drugstore, and drove in her Mercedes to meet her old friend, whom she hadn't seen since Bobby Kennedy was assassinated. They had been in their twenties, then, working for the Kennedy campaign in Boston. Kitty had been her friend since age nine. Now they were both nearly forty. Marcia was very conscious of this fact, and how rare it was to see and be seen by someone after years had gone by. She checked her face in the rearview mirror several times. More worn than usual, since the operation, she still had a healthy tan on conventional Anglo-Saxon features, a chiseled face which gave little expression, as if she had been instructed early that the best way to preserve beauty is to reserve all emotion for the voice, not the face.

Kitty, on the other hand, looked as if every one of those forty years had made a difference, as she stood on the sidewalk, holding the hand of her small, thin, red-haired boy. She wore a flowered shift, washed to dull sprays, flat sandals, and her hair—once famous for its flaming copper lights—was chopped short, had grown dark. She had no tan.

She helped her son into the back seat and climbed in beside Marcia. They gave each other one of those tense and fumbling embraces which signify duty, not heart, and smiled, at a distance, inspecting each other.

"You look great," said Kitty.

"So do you!"

"Ha!" Kitty smiled and lit up a cigarette. "I wish."

Marcia turned the car around and let out a sigh and a wince, so Kitty would know that she was in some pain and that gratitude was called for.

"Thank you for picking us up," said Kitty promptly, and she introduced her son, who only murmured a response.

"How many children do you have? I can never remember if it's three or four."

"Four," said Kitty. "Where are your two?"

"At camp, thank God, so I can get some work done."

"Work on what?"

"I write a regular monthly column for a magazine here. It has a small circulation but a good reputation. It makes me feel useful."

"Good for you . . . And Dan? How's he doing?"

"He was made a junior partner just two months ago. So we're great. Fine!"

Marcia's face shifted at the mention of her husband, just enough to let Kitty know there were problems.

At home, the little boy Andrew was given a sandwich and a television to watch in a cool room. Kitty wouldn't let him swim. He limped slightly, Marcia noted, and he said so little she wondered if he was spastic. Something about his skin quality—translucent and lightly freckled—or was it his poor teeth?—made her feel he couldn't belong to her old friend Kitty. He seemed like a stranger's child, off the streets, and not a child she would warm up to.

She and Kitty sat outside in the sun. And Marcia began at once to narrate, in a low breathless voice, the drama of her recent life. "I'm madly in love with this man," she said to the sun, "but he won't leave his wife, and he doesn't want me to leave Dan. It's a matter of security, which I really need, and which Dan does give me. Also, of course, because of the *children*. But it's driving me *mad*. We can only meet in seedy hotels, when I'm supposed to be going over copy or something, for the magazine. He's a writer, too—quite well known, so I won't mention his name."

Kitty said nothing, but sipped ice tea and smoked incessantly, her features tense.

"I can't tell you how I've suffered," said Marcia, and paused for a deep breath. "See, I went into the hospital to have an abortion. I didn't know whose child it was—his, or Dan's."

Kitty glanced at her. "Did Dan know this?"

"Lord, no!" laughed Marcia. "Are you *kidding?*"

"Would you have had the abortion if you had known whose child it was?"

"What a peculiar question. I don't know. It was horrible anyway, no matter what. And I got an infection afterwards. Agony!" Another sigh. "And Dan's furious at me for having done it. As if it was *his* baby. And I've had to lie about *that*. So I'm in a really deep depression."

"No wonder," said Kitty, but her voice was a little cool and distant.

Usually, at a certain marked age, a person transforms either physically or socially. Kitty had not changed that much physically—gone over the hill, as Marcia would say—yet. Her hair was dark but not gray, and her features, though scattered with impressions, were still the basic ones she had had from nine years old. But her manner had changed. She was abrupt, not fluid as she used to be; and she was nervous.

Marcia picked up on these facts, and eyed her old friend, cautiously.

"Remember," she said, "when we wore those red stars on our coats? Little Bolsheviks was what your mother called us. God, that seems long ago. I used to think your mother was the *epitome* of radical. And you, too . . . Tell me about where you live and what you do."

"In Riverdale, just outside Manhattan," said Kitty. "In an apartment. I'm on welfare."

"You're kidding." Marcia recalled Kitty's recent struggles to get through school while raising children. "Weren't you teaching or something?"

"Yes," said Kitty, "I was. I loved it. But, well, I'll do it again."

Kitty's voice was tremulous. She closed her eyes and face to the sun, as if she wished to become a stone dial. Marcia felt uncomfortable. She wondered why Kitty had come to Boston anyway, and then to see her. She had no family here anymore. Of course they were old friends, and they used to laugh, gossip, and agree on how awful everyone was. They even went South together during the civil rights movement. That's where Marcia met Dan; he was a young liberal lawyer in those days. And that's where Kitty met Lenny, who was more radical than any of them. Years later, after Kitty had had four children by him, he ran off with some left-wing Swedish woman, and never came back to America.

"Welfare," said Marcia quietly. "That must be hard."

"Oh well, it's temporary, I hope." Kitty turned her face now to look at Marcia's upturned profile, so Marcia missed the expression of dread that was on her old friend's features when she said, "Andrew is very sick. I wondered—wanted—to borrow some money from you, Marcia, so I can bring him to a specialist here at Children's Hospital. The Medicare doctors are okay, but not enough for me. I need to see someone else. The best. I have no one else to ask."

Marcia's expression changed only slightly, as her hands folded down on her abdomen; and then she let out a slight moan of pain.

"How much?"

"I'd need a thousand."

"You've got to be joking," said Marcia. "I can't possibly come up with that. A hundred maybe. But a thousand? I've got two kids in private school and now at camp. *God*. I'm sorry, Kitty, but no. I mean, after all, I've been going through hell, *too*. I just told you. I'm still weak as a *fish*. I can't have the man I love. I'm a *mess*. I thought you had just come to visit me. Out of friendship."

Kitty murmured, "I'd pay it back," and then said nothing. The sound of Woody Woodpecker came out of the television onto the close-cropped lawn.

Marcia couldn't bring herself to look at Kitty, so she imagined her instead. How her life must be. Four children in an urban apartment, poverty emanating from their persons as it did from the boy inside. She was angry. She thought of all the things Kitty could have done with her life. Not married Lenny—or stuck with him, anyway, for so many years, having children which she couldn't support. She somehow could have kept her job, or moved to a part of the country where she could take care of the children and get decent health insurance. She could have found herself another man. There were any number of paths she could have followed which would have led her away from squalor and, now, illness. And away from this occasion too.

Marcia heard Kitty stir and glanced aside to see her stand up and walk restlessly across the grass. She skirted the pool and stopped in the shade of the crab-apple tree, and looked around at the deep shrubbery and hazy bands of August light. With the sun behind her, even in her dreary little duster, Marcia noted that her friend gave off a kind of tension and energy that amounted to force.

Maybe, Marcia thought, Kitty was about to do something violent. Shoot her, and steal her jewelry or silverware. Pearls of sweat gathered on her lip and brow.

"More iced tea, Kitty?" she called in a high treble.

Kitty shook her head slowly and stared back across the grass at Marcia. Even the shadows had a dusty tone to them, as if they needed rain.

Marcia thought of apologizing to Kitty, of trying to explain her economic position in more detail, but the words, she knew, would sound false and contrived,

59

and Kitty would see through to what was really in her mind.

And what was really in her mind was her absolute conviction that the poor deserved to be poor, that there's no such thing as bad luck, no such quality as unequal opportunity, that Kitty was a perfect example of the failure of will which lies at the heart of poverty. This revelation—and such it seemed to Marcia—struck her with great clarity and lay behind her wild fear of Kitty at that moment. It was clear to her that they were enemies.

Just as Kitty began to move forward, the boy came out behind Marcia onto the patio. She jumped up quickly. He and his mother seemed to have a symbiotic relationship so deep that he knew he was ready to leave when she was. He walked out and met Kitty halfway, taking her hand and leaning in against her.

"The pool is so blue," Marcia heard him say, "you can't tell how deep it is."

"I know," said Kitty. "It's pretty, isn't it. Let's go, darling."

Marcia said, "You're leaving? So soon? I can drive you."

Kitty didn't protest. She followed Marcia over the thick shag carpeting into the front hall and out to where the car was parked. She climbed in the back seat with her son, and he began to talk, in hushed tones reserved for his mother, about the cartoon he'd been watching. This was a relief to Marcia because it meant she didn't have to make fake small talk. She pulled up where she found them, and Kitty got out of the car at once.

"Thank you," she said to Marcia, "for the drive," and then she took Andrew's hand and walked towards the trolley stop.

Marcia pressed the pain in her abdomen, watching them, and realized she had never even asked what was wrong with the boy, or if his illness might be fatal.

SCOURGE

WHEN HE SAW the lone girl he was in despair. *Mortal pain*, he told his sister. It was the sixties, if you know what I mean, and people were in a weird frame of mind. His friend had said the only people he knew who challenged racism were young white girls. But Joe didn't believe statements like that; he only believed in literature and his own emotions.

The girl was standing beside her car, and it came over him—as it never had before, but in a rush, like the fluid force of love—that he would go and take her purse away and have some money. He leaned against her—it was dark—and dislodged the shoulder bag easily. She didn't protest, but gave a look of blue-eyed anguish.

And he kept on walking. Why, I could have killed her and she wouldn't have said a thing!—a thought which scared him. How easy it was to do ill. What he had never done before from fear of consequence, had none. He held his pain around him like his coat, her purse under. Winter. The Shitty City is what he called Boston.

She called after him: "I didn't do anything to you!"

And he turned, so they saw each other's faces through the dark yards of cold air, and he started to argue, but went on instead, faster, as she entered one of the projects on the outer edge.

"Probably a social worker," he told Allen.

"You better watch out, your sister will beat the hell out of you, or report you, if she finds out."

Joan would, too; well, beat him anyway. Not report him. He allowed her the privilege of a whack, with a belt, across his bare back in the locked bathroom, when he stepped out of line. She had raised him, worked, went to law school at night, and he was only eighteen.

"Law is just for people with power," he quarreled.

"Not if the right people get hold of it," she protested.

"If you could tell me the difference between right and wrong, you wouldn't need the law."

"You tell me the difference."

He couldn't. He leaned under a lamppost, removing four dollars from the wallet, a glance at the ID, her name was Elaine, and threw the bag in the bushes. Then he wandered through the maze of projects, finally returning to the site, but her car was gone. Brick, cement, boarded-up windows, rats, and cold. Smoke came from his mouth when he sighed.

The difference between right and wrong: what was she doing over here anyway? Really it was too late for a social worker. They never hit after dark. She had no business in this territory, a young white girl: that made it her fault, and carrying a purse too. This reasoning confused him, returned the sadness he felt, out of nowhere, gloom coming, the way they say angels descend.

IT WAS A COUPLE OF WEEKS LATER when he met Elaine at a friend's apartment in the projects. She was a friend of his friend's sister, Isabel; they were both students at the same college. They were comparing notes in Ethics when he came in. Elaine looked really sick when she recognized him and started shoving her papers away.

"I forgot," she said, "I've got to go."

"Already?" Isabel sank back. "What for?"

"My father needs the car."

She stood up, dragging her coat and papers along. She didn't look at Joe again. "I'm sorry," she said. Isabel called to her brother, "Hey, walk Elaine out to the car."

"No, that's okay, he doesn't have to."

"After last time? You must be crazy." Isabel told Joe, "She got mugged."

"I'll walk her out," Joe said. "I've got my coat on."

"No—"

"Yes," said Isabel, "let him."

So the girl had to go with him. She went first down the dark green steps splashed with graffiti, trodding over smashed soda cans. She was rushing, no wonder.

"I'm not going to hurt you," he said.

She didn't look back, her long yellow hair bounced up and down. They stepped outside.

"It's definitely going to snow," he said. "The sky was yellow at six and now look at it."

Obediently she looked at it. From where they were positioned, they could see all the way to downtown Boston, gleaming bars of light like music across the black sky.

"Just keep walking," he said. "I'm not going to hurt you."

She walked, hurriedly, to her car.

"This time you're not carrying a purse. Still, it's weird you came back. Isabel a good friend?"

They looked at each other across the blue metal hood.

"I have a lot of black friends," she said earnestly. "But Isabel is the best."

He smiled, the way they always said something like

that, or made references to jazz, James Baldwin, or Marvin Gaye.

"Well, if you've got so many, how come you're so dumb about coming to a place like this? It's dangerous."

She got that look of blue-eyed anguish again, and his recognition of it made him feel he had raped, not robbed her. She was fumbling with the key—he didn't move, absorbing the bizarre nature of the situation, like a pleasure. He was now the danger and the protector; it had the irony of Greek drama—Sophocles' *Oedipus* he had always liked. Being two opposites combined, Fate. A new power. As she bowed her head to enter the car, he moved around.

"You can have another black friend, if you want."

"No, thanks."

"I'll pay you back."

"I already had to get a new license and credit cards."

"We can work it out." He smiled: "I mean, the economics."

She now had the door shut, and sealed inside, rolled the window a little down.

"This is insane," she said.

"Well, why not?"

She shrugged, rolled up the window, locked the door, and drove away.

HE HAD PAID HER BACK within a week. She drove him places, like to the factory where he stitched shoes, and to the library downtown, and to the two classes he attended at the state college. She would meet him on corners, and they never went near the projects together. She was twenty, and eager to please, playing only black music in the car and patiently waiting outside places. For some time they didn't touch but were bound by the sense of "recognition"—what had passed between them in the dark on that first night.

But finally one night she took him back to her place on Commonwealth Avenue; her roommate was gone for Thanksgiving, and they drank wine. She had long ash-blond hair, an ashy face which was long and serious, and good teeth. He looked her over, carefully, considering her appearance in terms of white teachers he had had. She was, like Isabel, bourgeois; not a hippy by any stretch of the imagination, she was neat and orderly, with respectable ambitions about being in early childhood education. All his girlfriends had been black, and he had never been serious, as they say. Just fooling around.

Now he was a little uneasy. She had told him about a boyfriend who lived with her once, but how it had disintegrated into petty quarrels and jealousies. He could sense that she had no knowledge of life's tragic side. She talked about bad things, but there was an emptiness to her vision that she clearly wanted filled. "It's really rough," she would say, about Life; or, "Sometimes I wonder." She expected that there should be solutions to problems and analyzable parts to evil. He did not.

He felt they came from different planets. But apparently she wanted something from him, some secret knowledge about danger, survival, and suffering; he felt this and shied away. His sister Joan called him "a walking mood" or "temper on legs." He was good-looking, too, in an almost Anglo way—light brown skin, aquiline nose, fine lips. It would be easy for her. Not so for him, though given their first meeting, there was an intimacy there already. So he didn't resist the obvious, and went to bed with her that night and many others.

JOE'S PAIN LIFTED SLIGHTLY, or for a short time. At least he now had some luxuries in his life like wine and a Volkswagen. They were reliefs from sullen drudgery, and hinted at some ultimate liberty, like bumping on walls which turn into doors.

He didn't introduce Elaine to Joan and made her promise to tell Isabel nothing either. He was embarrassed; he had a kind of image to protect around the projects, as one of the walking wounded—possibly brilliant, but who would ever know. And he couldn't help looking at other white women with curiosity; maybe it was true, they were more than just "liberal" and a good way to enter the free world.

"If you want to go out with someone else, just tell me," Elaine would say as he looked at women that way. Her jealous tone seemed strange to him, as they had made no commitments, no statement of love, and only, really, had a routine.

He responded by saying, "No, I'm okay," as if she had offered him coffee after dinner instead of another affair. It wasn't that he didn't care for her company. No one had ever listened so intently before to his eloquent, if bitter, ideas regarding race and poverty. Certainly no black woman would let him go on this way. She questioned him as if he were a young professor and listened, eyes glittering, with what could only be called fascination.

But so much of intimacy and confession went unsaid,

having no shared reference. Instead his words ran along a philosophical or visionary course.

"To be moral in an immoral society is literally impossible," he would say. "You are a fool, and destroyed, playing by different rules from the community you're in."

And Elaine, though she had studied ethics and political science, and knew a smattering of Marx and St. Augustine and all of Chekhov, had not experienced the loss of a moral center; and so she did not understand how it could make a person suffer. Morality and law were, in her mind, essentially the same. If you had not gotten caught doing something wrong, you were home free and need brood no further. For some reason, the blacks she knew even slightly, and those whose writings she had read, were obsessed by morality and justice in an inexplicable, rather terrifying way.

"The whole point of society," he would say, "is to remove natural inequalities. No one is created equal. That's what we've got to do when we make a society—create a false situation. One that is equal. I mean, even Mother Nature is a bitch."

IT WAS SNOWING. A great blizzard which might go on, like a Northeaster, for three days. What was the point of snow, Joe wondered; it didn't seem to do anything positive for the earth. It was irrelevant, unnecessary. This gave snow its fearful quality, and great draughts of unease passed through him in the dark, hearing it sift on the windowpanes. He wished he could really love the woman lying beside him, because then everything would be all right, so to speak. He would feel safe.

But he couldn't bring himself to love someone so alien, or since it would take so many years of struggle before he could, he might as well give up now and go home. Her sleeping face made him pity but not love her. He was empty of desire, and the proper thing to do, then, was leave; and he did quickly, with stealth, while she slept.

He went out into the depths of snow, wet on his face, deep in his shoes. No buses could plow through this, or cars. He realized he was a little crazy to do this and no one would understand, on a night like this, how he could choose physical suffering over physical comfort. She was warm in her bed, sleeping, and he hated the snow. But there was a certain beauty there, too, in the elephantine branches caking up, and the lights thrown out like sheets of gold silk along the residential snowy lawns. His feet were sore within minutes from cold and damp. No cars passed, but distant rumbles of snow plows reminded him he could take the subway home.

The word "scourge" entered his mind and he determined to look it up in his dictionary when he got home. On the subway, he took out of his pocket a copy of *The Magic Mountain* which he was in the midst of reading, and he swayed, cold, oblivious to those around him.

Unconsciously he knew his stop and got off, still reading, rising to the snow again, and now no trees, no bolts of gold silk, no Swiss mountains and Hans Castorp, but flat and desolate buildings, packed together, which struck him like a concentration camp or sanitarium, an exiled place for the hopeless or dying, and tears stung his eyes.

WHEN HE GOT HOME Joan was still up, studying at a coffee table in the living room. She was a heavy-set woman who bore no resemblance to him.

"What's wrong with you?" she asked after a glance.

"Just cold and wet."

"Well, why are you out in this weather? They even canceled my classes."

"Just wanted to come home."

He watched her, as she watched him removing his shoes and socks. His hair was glistening with snowdrops still.

"You've been seeing some white girl, I hear."

"Not any more."

"Allen told me. Don't know why."

He leaned his head back against the sofa and closed his eyes, and his sister looked at him with some compassion. She could only do this when he wasn't looking; it was like a stolen pleasure, or a sin, she never wanted him to know the extent of her concern for him. It might make him take advantage of her, as men will do if you let them know, was her experience.

"I told Allen I don't think it's such a bad idea," she said. "I mean it might be a way out for you."

The radiator hissed beside him. He opened his eyes partially to observe her, but she had returned her eyes to her work, and he felt chilled. It sounded like she was eager to get rid of him.

NO ONE COULD GO ANYWHERE the next day. The snow was still coming down. Joe lay with his book on the sofa, his bed in the living room, when Elaine called. She wanted to know why he left.

"To come home," he said.

"But I missed you."

She started to cry. He listened carefully, trying to figure out if she was faking or not. No words of comfort came to his lips, in case she was false. He stared at the window and the snow, listening.

"You don't want to see me any more," she said.

"Look," sitting up, "I don't think it's me you want, but some image."

"That's not true."

"Well then, what do you really want?"

"We could live together."

"Here?" he laughed.

"No. Here."

("It's one thing to find money, it's another thing to take it," his mother said years before.)

"We'd have nothing to lose," she went on, "by trying."

"I'm trapped," he said.

"By the snow?"

"Let me call you later."

She let him. He lay back with his book spread face down on him. He was weary of words and wished he could put the language in his mind to sleep. You could justify any action verbally, but it was all he seemed to do, or to make no action, really, just to fill the air with sound. With her mostly it felt like that. Imagining hours and hours of the same explanations, he yawned into his hand. *I can't live out there*, he said and realized he meant two things at once. Out there with his mouth, and out there in

74

those unfamiliar streets, with her. But he had pushed himself the other way by the force of this revelation.

He stood to look out the window, now ringed, pane by pane, with lips of snow. The snow drops were still small and fleet, which meant there was no relief in sight. The brick of the absorbing buildings had taken on some of the whiteness and seemed, he thought, half asleep. Yet outside children actually ran around, a few of them, some boys around ten and twelve. He knew they could be dangerous too, though young, and he remembered what he himself had done to Elaine.

His sister woke, emerged and asked who he was looking for. He told her no one and she stretched, eying him suspiciously, and returned to bed with a cup of tea and a notebook. Joe sat by the window, staring out, as the time drew on through hours; this was the way he was happiest, just staring and thinking, no one to bother him. He saw the kids plant rocks in snowballs under the shaft of the building's shadows and knew exactly how they felt about it.

Finally he called Elaine.

"The main roads are plowed," she said. "I can come get you."

"Give me an hour," he sort of sighed.

"I'm not forcing you."

"I know."

"Well, why do you sound like that?"

"I'm fine," and he cleared his throat. "But hey, tell me one thing."

"What."

"Do you love me?"

There was a pause before she cried, *of course!* whole-heartedly. He dropped his eyes to the telephone mouth-piece and drew in his chin with a smile.

"Okay. See you. Outside."

He was going to tell his sister where he was going, but dread sank into his hands as if he were holding two hard lumps of bread. He could call her, he figured, and let her know later.

So he filled two paper shopping bags with clothes and vital books by Dostoevsky and Rousseau—just about all he had. Then, without saying goodbye, he left, to meet her in the parking lot so no one would throw a stone at her head. He felt heavy with stories he had read about moves like this—slave stories about escape—and he guessed he would survive this way, by reference and by thought.

ELEVATOR STORY

A QUICK STORY. There was this man who had three wives, two of them former, living with him in a high-rise condominium in Boston. The apartment had been made out of two adjoining suites, and so there was plenty of space for four, or more.

The women were similar, physically, in a couple of ways only. Each was slightly plump, indicating a pleasing absence of vanity, and each was pale-complexioned. One, however, was very blond with thin baby-like strands of hair at the nape of her neck. She was the middle. The third, newest wife was dark-haired, with a thoughtful oval face and the flush of one who suffered from youthful acne. The first wife I liked best. She was small and silly, but clever with her tongue. She would joke, laugh and look at your response slyly. They were all in their thirties; it was 1983.

All three worked at various high-powered jobs during the day and returned at nearly the same time home at night. Usually they went everywhere he did, after work and on weekends, though not all of them went to bed with him at night. No. The new wife was his only lover. The rest were his friends.

He was a tall shambling man with strawberry-blond hair, a pale and ruddy complexion like the Irish, and a conventionally handsome face. Dreamy, though. You felt he never saw you at all! He rarely said anything, but smiled a little at jokes—especially those made by the first wife;

and he indicated no overt affection whatsoever towards his new wife. How did he keep them? This was the first question to cross your mind. And why did they all live together?

On the elevator you would hear them talk, and there was no question that the wives helped pay for the living quarters and food, and the man, a professor or something, also paid his fourth of everything. They were sensible, amiable, egalitarian, intelligent, and, I suppose, liberated from guilt because there was no trace of embarrassment regarding their situation.

Once, on a winter day, there was a fourth woman on the elevator with them. First they were assembled in the lobby waiting to go up. All were cold, booted, and sprinkled with a fairy glitter of melting snowdrops. The fourth woman was particularly shivery, the nervous type. She was small and emaciated, with a torrent of straw-colored hair tumbling halfway to her bottom.

The man stared at the moving column of numbers while the women chatted softly about their plans for a winter vacation.

"I think we should go and spend a week in New York—seeing plays, galleries, the works!" said the new wife.

The middle frowned, "Oooh. I'd rather go to California."

"And I want to go to the Caribbean," said the first wife, "and have piña coladas tubed into me while I scuba."

"How will you decide?" inquired the new woman in the group.

"We will—um—draw lots," said number one, "but that's fine. I mean, one thing is really as good as the next. Right?"

"I guess so," she said, "if you think that way."

The new woman looked at the man, whom she could see in profile. His gentle, amiable expression seemed to hold her attention. That is, she gazed at him with combined longing and concern, as if he were, perhaps, dying before her eyes, and if she stopped looking, he'd be gone.

The elevator arrived and the group got on. The women talked about the terrible plight of Boston school children, who read at third-grade level when they're graduating from high school. One of the women, the middle, was a teacher.

She said, "It's the lack of any motivation coming from home. Reading means nothing at all to children whose home life is devoted to television, no matter what the teachers tell them."

"Home life is crucial," the new woman stated, "for all growth."

"Growth?" number one said with a wrinkle of disgust. "I hate that word. It implies something completely false."

"What's that?"

"Well, that there's progress," she replied.

"And you think there isn't any?"

"None," she said flatly. "We go up, we go down. the causes for one or the other are unknown, as are the results."

Wife number two explained further, "She means that, sure, it's great that there are elevators, light bulbs, hot baths, and bicycles, but they don't imply progress, or growth, so much as, pure and simple, something new."

"Hmm," mused the new woman and her eyes were fixed on the man's long and shapely hands. "What's your profession?"

"I'm an engineer," the second wife said.

"Bizarre," murmured the new woman, and we all disembarked on the fourteenth floor.

SHE DID NOT MOVE IN WITH THEM, but began to hang around, coming alone at odd hours, when they would either buzz her up or pretend they weren't at home. If she was an irritant, they didn't let her know. She was a widely published poet whose highly formal work had won her a good deal of success in the local Boston scene.

"It's all timing. Everything is timing," the current wife said on the elevator one evening. "I go along with Thomas Hardy in that regard."

"Me too," her two friends agreed.

"Timing—whether you get the right job, the right house, the right husband—that's all it is."

"All the more reason to recognize what's right," said number one and she smiled and hugged herself tight. You had to like her, because she, and the other two, were without affectation. They were serious, good, committed women.

The man seemed the same. That was the strangest part, I suppose. You wanted him to be a tyrant or lecher and he wasn't. He helped button a glove; he let them off the elevator first; he picked up whatever one dropped; he carried and shopped for them. And all this, without losing dignity. Far from it!

The poet seemed to focus increasingly on him as the winter went by. They all went away without her—to Paris, as it turned out—and didn't answer her buzzes for a few days after their return. She kept coming back. I felt she

82

was more than prurient; the intensity of her interest in this happy group seemed to border on appetite. Especially when it came to him.

But the man paid her no more heed than he did anyone else. He was not flattered. He was polite, distracted, and rarely if ever looked at her. Yet it was his attention she was after. You knew that. ·

She cross-examined the women, when she was alone with them, waiting to go down one day.

"How do you all do it? Aren't you jealous?"

"Of what?" asked the new wife.

"Of him. Of each other."

"Those are different, and mutually exclusive emotions. How can you be jealous of him and each other at the same time? It's impossible."

She laughed with her friends.

The poet persisted: "People must ask you questions. Your families must wonder. It's not exactly common, you know."

"Oh well," sighed the funny one, "it's six of one, a half dozen of the other."

The poet was mystified by this remark. And it's here that the story picks up speed. The poet was in love with the man. The women knew it, and didn't appear bothered. When she wasn't there, however, they lashed into her poetry, whispering how mediocre it was, and how predictable formally, and how lucky she was to have been born a poet at the right time and in the right place for mediocre poets. But they didn't say anything else mean about her. On the contrary. They praised her clothes, looks, and her ability to live alone.

She got him alone on the elevator one day. He was pulling a cart of groceries. In front of everyone there, she fell against his body and buried her face in his coat, and begged him to love her the way he loved them. She was sobbing and drooling like a small child, and he brushed her off with remarkable grace, wiped off her lips and cheeks with his handkerchief, and she was reasonably composed by the time they reached their floor. It had all happened quite fast, in other words, as bad timing is apt to do.

What happened after, I don't know. She didn't stay long; the others said she was the kind of woman who hates a man who doesn't love her. In fact, we never saw her again after that. However, soon after, she published a poem in free verse which few could understand for its surreal allusions and leaps; but the little group understood. They were delighted she had written something strange and new. They were not, after all, jealous of success or each other, but honestly hoped that others would do their very best. She should have known that.

The man chose his wives well, you have to admit, and so did they.

LOTTO

LIKE MOST EVERYONE I know, the less money I've got, the more I spend on beer, cigarettes, and lottery tickets. Call it what you will, but I say the harder the life, the more you spend on junk. However, one time, I have to admit, I went a little too far with that last particular chance, and ended up where I least expected to.

It was Sunday morning when Bobbie, my ex, called at his usual time. For eight years I'd thought we were separated, since we lived in different places, but he seemed to think this arrangement was only a matter of convenience. He called, frequently, "just to check," and appeared at all hours to visit the children.

This call came about two hours before I was going to drag everyone off to mass. It was a beautiful morning: soft autumn air, gold leaves on the pavement, that haze of the last days of summer around the borders of the trees. The girls were already complaining about being stuck in church for an hour, and the boys were banging a basketball up and down outside as if it was a punching bag.

Bobbie said, "Don't laugh."

"Why would I?"

"I just found one of those instant lotto games in yesterday's mail. And I scraped the little circles with a penny and came up at the top of the pyramid."

"That's a first," I said. "What does it mean?"

"I either win a Cadillac, $20,000, a color TV, or a home computer."

"I bet."

"It's true, Peg. Let me read it. There's a hitch."

"There's always a hitch."

"Well, actually there are two. One, I have to drive all the way to Cape Cod to collect . . . And two, I have to bring my wife along. The deal is supposedly for Young Marrieds."

"We certainly don't fit in that category, Bobbie. I think you better give it up."

"Are you kidding? I'm at the top of the pyramid!"

"You're not a Young Married, Bobbie. You know that."

"I can pass for thirty-five. People always say that to me. Besides, you know—for the kids. Whatever it is, I'll give it to the kids."

"The Cadillac? The money?"

"I'll sell the car," he said, "and pay off some debts and I'll give the rest to you and the kids."

The trouble was, he'd probably do it. I knew that from experience. He'd split the money between me and the kids and him, and then he'd be poor again—which seems to be the way he likes to be anyway. Ever since we broke up, he hadn't made a dime. It was like the way you can sail around with an anchor on board ship, but throw it over, and neither one of you moves. Nothing had changed for either of us since we separated.

"I don't want to get involved," I told him. "Bye now."

I hung up. Lots of times I didn't even say bye but slammed it down in his face. It didn't faze him. In an hour, he was outside the house in his truck. He got Tony to bring me the lotto card inside. Bobbie was not allowed through my garden gate since he pitched a tent in the front yard and wouldn't move. He called himself a squatter and had the children bring him plates of food. For two months I couldn't get him off my property—him and his dog and his portable john from the construction site where he was then working.

I stood in the kitchen and read the card. The top of the pyramid belonged to Bobbie all right. The numbers he had scraped matched.

I told Tony to tell his father, "Go to the Cape and see what you can get."

Tony ran out. Then in again.

"He says you have to go with him," he told me, his brown eyes focused on a blister on the palm of his hand, not me.

"Ha! Tell him he better plan on going alone or finding someone else to pretend she's his wife. I'm not going anywhere with him."

"I'll tell him." Tony ran out; then his little brother, Dunky, came in.

"Daddy says you don't have to drive in the truck with him. You take your car and he'll follow you. Then you can collect the prize and just leave. Come on, Mom, do it!"

"Why can't he do it alone?"

"I'll find out again," said Dunky and shot out the door.

I watched them all conferring by the gate which leaned, broken, under the weight of Bobbie's arms. The girls had gone out to get involved too, both of them bigger than me, in full make-up and half-dressed for mass. There was a circle of trees and berries around them, like a wreath, and outside that circle the hazy tenements stretched flat against the blue sky like perforated cardboard. I heard a siren and automatically counted the heads outside.

The oldest, Sue, came into the house to give me the next installment.

"Go, Mom," she said. "All you have to do is pretend you're still married. No big deal. I'll take everyone to mass. Go on! You'll be alone for a while. Won't that be nice?"

Sue grinned seductively at me, then inserted the details into this fantasy which would trap me.

"Just think!" she said, "You, alone in your car, with the radio blasting, driving to Cape Cod! And maybe at the end, you'll pick up a fortune. Oh Ma, go on."

It was the radio part that got me. I love to drive alone with my car radio. I could have told her, in one minute, the list of things I would do with that money: the roof, the basement, the fence, and some rooms. Then we would sell the house for three times its original value and get the hell out of Boston. She knew all that already.

"He says for you to call the people and tell them you'll be there at two," called Rachel.

I went to the door and looked past the bunch of them at his large, bent frame. He was wearing an Army jacket, work boots, and faded jeans. A balding pear-shaped Irish head, a face I hadn't seen close up since he pitched the tent eight years ago.

I shouted out, "We'll never pass for Young Marrieds, and don't you dare lay a hand on me. I'm not your wife!"

"Don't worry, Peg," he called back with a smile. "All we want is the present, right? They have to give it to us."

90

"This is insane," I told myself and plowed through the books of food stamps in my bag to get to my car keys. I was as badly dressed as he was, in my jeans, old sneakers, and the dirty blue sweatshirt I always wear around the house.

I called the number on the back of the card and a spry female answered my suspicions, saying, "If you keep your appointment, you get your gift. Just like it says."

I told her two o'clock and kissed my kids goodbye. They rowed up along the fence to watch, their expressions both cynical and jokey. They thought it was a riot that we were pretending to be married still, and had no faith that we'd come back with the money. Just a little hope was all.

I DROVE AHEAD OF HIM through the neighborhood. He was driving his truck. A couple of people waved to us and watched, with surprised looks, as we passed. This was the neighborhood we both grew up in. And it was Bobbie's big idea that buying our house would lead to security, because of all the renovation going on around us. In fact, we missed "gentrification" by two blocks. And our house still stands in a rundown block of wooden tenements fifteen minutes away from downtown Boston. Bobbie does occasional carpentry work on the Victorian mansions nearby, just to keep himself going. Meantime, I'm a full-time secretary, and when I'm not burning out my brain cells over a word processor, I'm killing my boss mentally. Resentment I can't seem to get rid of.

Except, that is, when I'm on the road. Then I'm happy. Once we got out of the nasty battleground of Boston's shabbier neighborhoods and into the green hills of Milton, I felt my spirits lift. I blasted the radio, sang along, and noticed, through the rearview mirror, that Bobbie looked pretty happy too, with his dog Bruno sitting up front beside him. Bobbie lived with his sister and her family. They're all teetotalers and TV addicts.

I forgot about Bobbie for most of the drive, which was just about the most exciting trip I'd taken in ten years. Two hours of solitude! And I hadn't been down to the South Shore for about that long, and not to the Cape since I was a kid. I rolled down the window and let the wind blow my eyes into a squint and had all these fantasies about coming back to Boston rich enough to leave. When we climbed over the Sagamore Bridge and crossed the canal, I was about as high as I ever get, even on beer.

I had the direction for Gray Waves, the place we were going, on the back of the card beside me. It was located on the inner Cape, somewhere near Falmouth, which meant we left the big highway soon and drove down a pretty narrow road. I was thinking—my mind was racing—about how dangerous the city is for kids, and how marriage is an impossible institution. If you thought of a man and a woman as two halves of a whole, it was probably better, because putting the two halves together made sense. But when you thought of a man and a woman as two complete wholes, there was no way you could put them together anymore.

I could smell the sea somewhere though the scrubby pine trees that lined the road and I began to look for the sign to Gray Waves. Bobbie was tailgating me and I waved my arm and gave him the finger and he backed off. Gray

Waves turned out to be a resort: modern saltboxes, tennis courts, and a half-full parking lot. A mystery.

We parked beside each other. Bobbie let the dog run off into the woods to pee and we stood, at a distance from each other, to talk.

"How are we going to do this?" I asked.

"Hell, I don't even know what it is," he said.

"There must be an office or something."

"Well, I'll stay here with Bruno. You go check and see what we do. You've got the card."

"And you've got to be kidding. I'm not going to do all the work. I'll stay with the dog. You find out what's happening."

Bobbie shrugged nervously and took the card from me. He didn't like dealing with strangers, but neither did I.

"I can lock the dog in the car," he said, "and you come with me."

"No. I'll take him for a walk."

"But I'm supposed to be here with my wife."

"Tell them she's walking the dog."

"He doesn't bite," said Bobbie, and off he went with the card.

I set off along the border of the woods, calling Bruno to follow. On my left the settlement emerged from the trees like a Hollywood set. People were ambling along little lanes in front of the houses, all dressed up as if for a work day or a dinner out at the country club.

I jogged down a sandy road into the woods. There's a special Cape Cod smell I knew from childhood and it knocked me into a shock of nostalgia. The smell is like a hot baked blueberry leaf, sort of bitter and sweet together.

I paused to inhale it, and tears came into my eyes. It was like burying my face in a familiar neck, and I stood, breathing deep, and nearly weeping while the dog barked into the trees.

Then I heard Bobbie calling my name, and the feeling went away.

He was waiting at the road's end with a dark-haired young woman; she was crisply dressed in a white middy shirt and a pleated skirt and heels. Big breasts and a big pink mouth, all smiles. I thought Cadillac and went forward.

"This is my wife," said Bobbie. "Peg, this is Gwen."

Gwen was a genius of pretense. You would never have known from her manner that Bobbie and I looked like a couple of street-cleaners compared with the other "visitors." The dog's nose went for her crotch and she slipped her hand under his jaw and giggled. Bobbie grabbed Bruno.

"The dog can't come inside the office," said Gwen, as if it made her sad.

"I'll put him in the car for a while," he said and left me alone with Gwen's small talk.

"Did you have a comfortable drive down, Peg? Your husband says you both come to the Cape whenever you can, and the children just love it here. I grew up just down the road myself and I'm still here. I'll never leave Cape Cod . . ."

I had no idea what was going on and when I saw Bobbie returning, I gave him the same look I give my boss. He averted his eyes and called to Gwen: "Well, now, where do we get our gift?"

She laughed and shook her head, "Not yet! Not until you've listened to my spiel!" Another giggle at the audacity of her role as a trap.

We had definitely fallen into some kind of trap, and I didn't like it.

"What spiel? What's this all about?" I asked.

"Well, that's for you to find out," she said and turned herself around and aimed for the building beside the tennis court. "Come on!"

"How long will it take?" I asked.

"That depends on how interested you get and how many questions you ask."

She led us through the office and out into a glassed-in lounge—classy with butcher-block tables, and styrofoam cups of coffee; it looked into a row of golden branches and paths leading to the saltboxes. There were couples of all ages at the other tables, conversing with guides like Gwen, and dressed for whatever the occasion was. Bobbie and I sat down while Gwen went off to get some papers.

"What the hell," I whispered at him, "are we doing here?"

"I don't know. Waiting to get a Cadillac, I guess."

"It's a lure."

"Just play along."

"What if they find out we're legally separated. Huh?"

"They won't," he said and fumbled with pack of cigarettes uncertainly. No one else was smoking.

Gwen came back with packets of materials about Gray Waves. It turned out to be a condominium development which had failed, and was now, under new management, a time-sharing racket. You were urged to invest in the property, which would give you a two- or three-week vacation slot in one of the houses. Gwen wanted to give us every detail on the advantages of this investment.

Bobbie said, "I know all about it," and blew smoke in her face. "You don't have to tell me anything."

"How do you know all about it?" she asked politely.

"Hell, I work in construction. I know what's going on in real estate." He was proud of himself.

"I bet you don't know about our bonus deal here at Gray Waves." She pulled a large glossy booklet out from her pile, and smiled at me. "Where do people like you like to go on vacation?"

"Bed," I said.

A laugh. "No, I mean, where would you want to go?"

Bobbie yawned.

"You, Bob, where have you traveled?" she asked, trying to jolt him awake.

"Korea," he said, "and before that, Ireland. Before we were married."

Gwen talked about the beauties of Cork and Wicklow while Bobbie moved restlessly in his chair. We could hear the dog barking from the truck all the way in the parking lot.

"When do you come to the Cape?" Gwen asked him.

Now he had to lie in front of me, and he looked at the ceiling and said, "Oh, we come down in the summer, on weekends, you know, to swim, that's all. I'm worried about my dog."

"You can get the dog when we're finished here," she told us.

I saw ourselves through her eyes: a pair of low-class slobs with four kids and no common sense or style. Pigs.

A mess-up on the computer list she must have got our names from.

"Where did you get our name from?" I asked her. "What list?"

"I'm not exactly sure," said Gwen, "but whatever it is, it shows you're good citizens with good credit."

Bobbie and I glanced at each other, and tensed against a laugh. His credit rating was zilch and I couldn't even get a Sears card.

"Well," she hurried on, "the incredible bonus you get from buying into Gray Waves is that you can travel almost anywhere in the world and stay for only forty-two dollars a night in a first-class hotel suite big enough to accommodate your whole family . . . Look."

She passed Bobbie the big picture book, showing hotels in cities from Paris to Capetown.

"I wouldn't want to invest in South Africa," said Bobbie, who never forgets his politics. He's a dyed-in-the-wool Kennedy Democrat.

"You wouldn't have to go there. You could go to Paris, say, or Nice, where I went last year."

"That sounds fine," I said, "but I'd sort of like to see what you've got right here."

"Listen," she said, her natural color pushing through the rouge spots. "I can tell you're impatient to see what your gift will be. Want me to get it now, and then you can listen to me?"

"Can't we just get it and split?" asked Bobbie.

"I'm afraid not, Bob," she said. "Peg, you want me to go get the gift?"

"Why don't you just show us the place here and talk at the same time," I said.

Gwen grinned at Bobbie. "You two must be real compatible. Always in a hurry. Right?"

"She's just eager to see the place here," he said. "And I want to get the dog out of the damn truck."

"All right, but I hope you understand the deal I'm describing to you. It's a once-in-a-lifetime opportunity, and after today there won't be any more space in this, the last resort of its kind on Cape Cod. Believe me. For two or three weeks of vacation a year, you pay very little. And you can always sell your share in a year or two for a substantial profit."

"Can I get my dog?"

"Go ahead, but keep him on a leash, Bob," said Gwen and she led me out the glass doors into the open air. People were still milling along the paths like graveside visitors on Memorial Day.

"Can I peek into one of the houses?" I asked.

"Let's wait for Bob, Peg," said Gwen and leaned against a tree to look at her nails.

I stared down the lane bordering the modern condominiums. They were designed like almost every other building going up around town: lots of glass and gray unfinished wood. The roofing slid down at a long sharp angle, and you could bet there was solar heating involved in the shape of the thing. New grass had been laid down, not raised from somewhere under the earth, and the trees were freshly planted, weak little things. All I could think was, *It's not fair*. Then I saw Bobbie coming along with the dog, his large lumbering body the only familiar sight around, and he was smoking again.

Gwen started us off towards the model open house, and

asked, "What did you think of Korea, Bob? We have a hotel there, too—in Seoul. Was it as exotic as they say?"

"I didn't get off base all that much, and when I did, I hated it. The Koreans are racist, for one thing. And the food is made out of dogs, cats, and rats. Half my buddies had to stay behind in a hospital because of a special strain of VD they caught, and they're still there, locked up for life."

"Wow, that's too bad," she said vaguely, and we crossed over the flagstones past an outdoor pool. She explained that it stayed warm nine months of the year. "Solar heat!" she exclaimed and opened a door onto an indoor pool, "for the three months when it's too cold . . . And indoor courts, too."

The dog, as nondescript as a pile of old autumn leaves, was not used to being on a rope. He was pulling Bobbie along and gagging and drooling from the tension around his collar.

"Your kids should've come along. They might have persuaded you to grab this chance while it's here," said Gwen. "You've got four? That's a lot. Must be expensive too."

"It is," I said and gave Bobbie a mean glance.

"But you both work?"

"Yeah, both of us work," he said.

"Well, of course you two might just want to go on a little vacation alone . . . to one of those foreign places. Get away from the kids for a few days? Nice idea, Peg? You said you like to spend your vacation in bed," she added in a tone I couldn't interpret. I wanted to get away from her, soon, before I said something we'd all regret.

She paused outside one of the houses, and Bruno drooled on her shoe as she spoke.

"I want you guys to see a real short movie inside here. It will give you more of an idea of the deal we've got here at Gray Waves."

"I can't. I've got the dog," said Bobbie.

"Oh yes you can. I'll stay with him," she insisted.

We were shut, then, in a small room with movie chairs facing a television screen. The background music was Patti Page singing "Old Cape Cod." Bobbie sprawled two seats away from me, relaxing, I figured, at the sight of the familiar screen.

"This is the last time I ever listen to one of your dumb ideas," I said.

"Sorry, Peg, but it's not over yet. A Cadillac?"

"Big joke."

"Well then, why did you come?"

I watched these tan young bodies waterskiing and slurping down lobster on the screen.

"I guess I had some hope of winning." And I still had some, but didn't say so. Instead I suggested, "Maybe this is a good investment if you're someone with money. I mean, you have to admit, the place is pretty."

"It's a racket. What you're really doing is putting your money into some fat Wall Street company, as an investment for them. Pure capitalism. You pay two thousand dollars into their till, then make monthly payments, and you get two weeks time back. Big deal. It would be cheaper for us to rent a shack in New Hampshire for a month. And we wouldn't be surrounded by these Bermuda shorts and alligator shirts."

"What do you mean 'we'? I'm getting out of here," I told him and I opened the door. Gwen was standing guard with Bruno.

"The film's not over yet, Peg. Go back inside."

I did what she said. Bobbie was grinning.

"It's not funny," I told him. "We're being bullied by a girl who could be our daughter."

"But what if we get the color TV at the end? Even that would make this worth it, right?"

"I should've stayed home."

I thought of us sitting there, both in our forties, all fallen apart, the way Gwen would think about us.

"I guess you didn't need to come after all," he said. "She doesn't care if we're legally together or not."

I looked at his face close up. Naturally it was more lined than when I saw it last. So was mine. When we were kids in high school, he was considered a catch because he was good looking, though no one but me expected him to amount to much. I was wrong. He dumped the last bit of capital we had into some scam to do with importing rugs from Mexico, and we never recovered. We split up, figuring me and the kids would do better without mistakes like that.

"Let's get out of here," he said.

Gwen didn't push us back this time, because Bruno was beginning to howl like Caruso. She led us, instead, to the model home and let us bring the dog inside. The place was like something out of *House Beautiful*—wall-to-wall carpeting, a fireplace, pull-out couches, and two bedrooms and baths. Fresh linen daily. Silverware and china built into the cabinets.

"These come with your foreign hotel suites too," she said.

Bruno scratched, heartily, at some fleas on his belly and Bobbie looked like he was going to explode.

"We better get the dog outside," I said, and we all poured out into the sun again.

"What do you think?" Gwen asked.

"We'll have to think it over," I told her.

"I'm sorry, but there's no time to think," she said. "The place is almost full to capacity. If you want to come back to the patio, I can give you more information."

"I wish you hadn't tricked us like this," said Bobbie.

"It's no trick, Bob. You'll get your gift."

"It's a trick, a trap, a publicity racket, it should be illegal," he continued.

"Peg, stop moving away from me," Gwen snapped.

"Hey," said Bobbie, and gave her a filthy look.

"It's just that you guys are making the biggest mistake of your lives," she continued, placid again. "Why, *Reader's Digest* had an article not so long ago, showing why ninety percent of the people in this country own twenty percent of the wealth, and why twenty percent of the people own ninety percent of the wealth."

"Really?" said Bobbie, alerted. He loved that kind of talk which could only lead one way: to politics. And he seemed to think she was about to turn into a woman of the people, a spokesperson for the poor. His face warmed towards her.

"You want to know what the article proved?" she asked, excitedly.

"Yeah, go on," he urged her.

"It's the failure to make a decision that keeps ninety percent of the people down," she said, "a failure to make a decision. That's all."

Bobbie stared at her as if she had just turned into Richard Nixon.

"A failure to make a decision," he repeated. "Which decision? Which decision did they fail to make?"

She sort of slid back a step and into her smile.

"Come on Bobbie," I said. "Let's go."

"I want my present," he told Gwen, "if you'd please go get it."

"I'll get it," she agreed quickly.

"I bet it's one of those home computers, fifty bucks after Christmas, and if you damage them, you can't fix them because they don't make any replaceable parts. I just bet."

"Why would you be so sure, Bob?" asked Gwen. "This is a lottery. Keep your fingers crossed while I go see what it is."

We watched her go with none of our fingers crossed.

"I know it's the computer. It's rigged." He kicked the dust, and the dog snapped at a bee. "It should be illegal."

He looked down the row of houses, then at me. We both were breathing kind of hard, because deep down we both expected her to step out with an envelope containing a check for $20,000, or to call us around back where a long white Cadillac was parked and waiting.

"It can't be rigged," I told him. "That would be illegal."

He laughed and looked at me like I was about twelve years old.

"Never mind," he muttered. "You like this place? I can borrow from the family and get you and the kids set up here for your summer vacations."

"Don't be dumb, Bobbie."

"I could do it. I can make a decision like anyone else."

"No, don't. I hate Cape Cod."

"How can you hate Cape Cod?"

"It's easy. The smell or something. Makes me sick."

"But the kids might like it."

"No, they all hate it. Believe me."

"All right. If you're sure."

"I'm sure."

We watched the people making decisions under the shadows of the houses and the dog tugged on the leash. Gwen came back with our home computer which Bobbie let me carry, since I was bringing it back to the kids at home. She made one last remark about how compatible the two of us were. And then in the parking lot, we split apart, and he sped ahead. Just north of Plymouth, I slowed down. There was Bobbie by the side of the road. His radiator was sending up steam. We got some water, poured it in, and I ended up tailing him all the way back to Boston. So much for escape. On the way home, I was thinking about failure, if I was what they call one, or if Bobbie was.

Soon after this trip, we got back together.

THE COLD WAR

HE WAS SAID TO BE in the plumbing business, but no one there actually knew if it was true. He had a wife who stayed home and three children under ten who came with him that day. In the rooms, fragile by virtue of age and objects valued for generations, his presence was immense. Everyone aimed for the garden as soon as he came, passing by portraits and Irish landscapes. The man proceeded by them all without pausing while the American woman stopped in front of one picture after another.

Outside she looked at him. She had not been in Dublin before, or long. One week. She received the mysterious smells and sounds, like burning turf and church bells, passively. The huge handsome man in his shabby tweeds and muddy shoes called up a greater spirit in her, however. She couldn't stop watching him as he played with his cigarette in his large fingers before lighting it. She seemed eager to ask him questions, but the others there had his attention first. These were three very old women and one old man, all of them chain-smoking and drinking whiskey. The women didn't look a person in the eye, but conveyed intimacy by leaning close to speak while addressing the floor or some distant object. They each stole glances at the man.

If I wasn't an old hag, I'd go right for him, one of these women whispered huskily to the American.

Ah well, sighed the elderly gentleman, overhearing. You are an old hag.

THEY SAT, NOW, IN THE GARDEN, on white wrought-iron chairs, with drinks. An earlier rainfall had left a silver glitter on all vegetation, as if it were dawn. They were placed to gaze on an extraordinary array of flowers and herbs. These included tied and tidy rose bushes, strawberries, sweet peas in gentle pastels and climbing rods, fuschia, thyme, tarragon, and lavender. The garden was hidden by high walls; on the other side of one you could see the tops of trees with apples on them, hard red-brown objects like dollhouse fruit. The five children were staring greedily up at them, and clutched sacks full of used stuffed animals between them.

The plumber was too large for the chairs and sat on a stone embankment, politely listening to conversation while the children roamed along the edge of the wall, looking up. They were all only together by chance, and were not the types destined to meet often. The gathering was all for the children, who had made friends on the sidewalk outside, playing. The American children were not completely white. The Irishman asked their mother why.

Their father's from Columbia—in Latin America, she said.

Oh! Does he go back there often? asked the plumber.

Well, he's there when he can be. It's dangerous these days, you know.

I certainly do, the man said with a thrust of pleasure in his voice, suggesting camaraderie. I've just come back from North Africa myself.

Really. What were you doing there?

Business. And what do you do in America?

I'm a buyer.

Is that why you're here? he asked as if she were joking. To buy?

No. I'm just visiting my old friend—Moira, there; Mrs Hale. You must know her. You're neighbors.

They both looked at Moira Hale, an ancient elf of a woman, but under a heavy gray cardigan, whose house and garden these were.

No, I don't really, he confessed. My wife does.

Well, she's an old friend. She married an American professor who taught where I went.

What did he teach?

Literature, Irish and British. I've wanted to come here for years—to see what Joyce was writing about.

Ah, then this is your first time here?

In Dublin, yes. But I've been all over Europe and to Latin America too, natch.

You could see him examine her, then, with that expression of camaraderie that had given him a moment's pleasure. She was very pretty and leggy. Her blond hair was neatly folded back with barrettes and her wide mouth turned up at the corners, where light lines indicated humor. But her eyes were oddly hard, gray as ball-bearings.

What's the difference between a saint and a martyr? the old gentleman asked no one in particular.

I don't know, Billy, said Moira.

A martyr is married to a saint, Dear, he roared.

The plumber smiled, but still watched the American, who was looking at their children meandering around the grass cut as short as a shag rug. Her children were slim and dark, like formal twins, while his were a variety of gawky freckles, red-heads, and brunettes. His were boss-ing hers into some game involving fallen apples and stuffed animals.

They're all right, said the plumber with a nod at the children.

Yes. Mine love to be bullied.

Where did you say you went? called the elderly man. Africa?

Yes, that's right, he said.

I always wanted to go there myself! My father was sta-tioned for ten years in Nigeria. He loved the people.

Is that so, said the plumber.

He said Africans were the kindest people he ever came upon. He was with the British.

Ah yes . . . Well, I was on my own, actually.

You were on business you said? Where?

Well, in Algeria, Morocco. I would go to Capetown if I could.

When he said this, he lit his cigarette and took a long, tense drag—as if to muffle his next words, or to relax him-self. It was hard to say which, but he eyed the woman as if she might understand some piece of code he had just uttered.

Capetown? she said. There's supposed to be some beautiful and quite cheap property for sale there.

The plumber leaned back, then crossed forward over his legs again, nodding and exhaling, hard. His skin tone seemed to shift and he automatically checked the sky, as if it were a mirror.

They don't, in America, talk much about apartheid, do they?

Not really, no, she replied.

Why is that?

I suppose because of the whole race issue we've got ourselves. Let sleeping dogs lie?

Yes, I suppose. Still it would seem, I mean, you're not Europeans . . . So why cover for the Afrikaaners?

Money, I guess. The mines etcetera.

King Solomon was black.

Everything is money. My husband is in business, like you. But it's his father's company. In Bogota. His life has been threatened more than once. Terrorists . . . My husband does a little work for the CIA.

I personally, said one of the old women ardently, I personally believe that war is for the middle-aged . . . And I also don't think that one can be a conscientious objector without being a protector of the status quo.

Everything to do with money—with numbers!—has to do with evil, *is* evil. Have you noticed that? asked Moira, generally.

The third old woman caught this observation, as if with her hands. She was a white witch, it turned out, and looked like one, as she talked about numerology and Aleister Crowley. Her chin almost touched her nose, she had so few teeth between. She waved two sets of fingers in the air before her.

Numbers can be very good too, she said mildly.

But I agree about money, the big Irishman asserted. It is a deep affliction for the human race.

THE GATHERING HAD BEEN BILLED as a tea party, but there was no tea. The American woman held her empty

111

glass to the Irishman on his way for general refills. When he disappeared inside, the women instantly began to whisper, while the odd man out, folding and unfolding his legs, stared into the garden.

How could he have been to Africa? A plumber?

They make a fortune. He said he's in business.

Oh well, he's terribly handsome.

And his wife is as dull as bones. I've seen her.

He's lively. I like him myself.

I'm not so sure.

Why not? asked the American.

Something doesn't fit, said Moira, but I don't know what it is. He's very worldly.

And when he returned, two of the old women beamed and the third murmured, Ah, virility, as he handed her a new drink.

THE PLUMBER CONTINUED, then, to talk to the American, but not so freely. She threw questions at him now, in the spirit of a journalist, and he began to withdraw by listening in on the conversations of the old.

Americans never admit how much money they have, said the witch, because, I think, of the Puritan ethic. They're ashamed of any sort of padding. They want to feel they are the fittest, if only the fittest can survive . . . Am I wrong?

No, I think you're right, the old man replied. I once knew a businessman from San Francisco. He came here to fish every summer for years. The story about him goes that he once spent a week trying to catch a salmon. On the seventh day, he did, but by then he was in a rage, of course, at all the time he'd lost and the money . . . On the way back to the hotel, he growled at his fishing guide, "For God's sake, one salmon has cost me six hundred pounds!" And the fisherman replied, "It must be a very good salmon then, to cost so much."

They all laughed, especially the plumber. But there seemed to be a political side to the story that the American woman missed, because while she laughed, her gray eyes were cold and panicky.

I'm from Boston, she said, and my husband has connections through his business with people in Belfast. What do you think is going to happen in the north?

At first there was silence; then the plumber volunteered a response: It's still in the dialectic stage. Which is unfortunate.

In Boston they say nothing can happen till the British leave, she went on . . . Dialectic? What is your business?

I'm a buyer too . . . Ammunition, she thought she heard him say, and then he began to laugh at a story the old fellow was telling now, and which he followed as if it were a kind of instruction. It was, however, just a worn joke about a priest asking an unwed pregnant woman, "Are you sure you're the mother?"

AMMUNITION? AMBITION? The American got up, the way people do when they're upset, to look at the children present and invent some warning to send out to them.

The plumber did the same. And the two of them stood side by side, facing the garden, where the children moved animals among themselves and spoke in strange voices. The two parents said nothing. Meanwhile, behind them, the old ones were laughing and exchanging stories. And you would have thought the two in the middle had once had an affair, their silence was so heavy within the pleasures of the others.

GRAY

SHE STOOD IN THE STREET, perplexed, as if she had just been dropped there. This was the late 1900s in a Western European city much like any other, where the streets at lunch hour teemed with office slaves like herself, with their sandwiches slightly wet from sitting in ice all morning, and most of each month a cloud would cover the city, immovable and oppressive, wet all the way down to the pavement, wet in the fumes of buses and trucks slamming inches from the face.

She had gotten a temporary job working for an academic institution because of her nearly paranormal skills on a computer. Her hatred for the computer was part of her professional objectivity in dealing with their programs and systems. Sometimes the desire to kill a thing produces the profoundest understanding of it; it creates a powerful spell. Even now she was suffering from the inability to leave her computer work behind; to stop hating it and forget the case her boss had just dropped on her. She could not enjoy her lunch break.

What had happened was this. They were standing in the two-tiered office off a busy street that morning. The boss, a professor, and the office worker were both American, but he had a long-haired and sloppy look, along with a soft voice that somewhat masked his nationality. She wore the international student apparel that travels like mercury and her hair to her earlobes.

"While you are updating the system, I want you to keep your eye out for an error in there," the professor said. "It might be in the data base. It might be human fallibility. The problem has existed for three years, so you have masses of material to plow through—three hundred files for each of those three years. And two different programs. But don't be daunted. The error is there somewhere."

"Why," she asked him, "is this so important? One error in three years is inevitable." She had never been asked to locate an error before; and now it upset her.

"True, but our system is archaic. And the problem relates to a grade a woman received during the first year she was here and which is affecting her entire career. She will sue the institute—or bring us to court at least—if we can't prove that our grade was based on solid evidence."

"What kind of solid evidence?" she asked.

He explained—in the patient but remote tones of an academic—that the student, who had come over from America for one year, had received an A in a certain class. This excellent grade had given her the impetus to pursue a course of studies on her return to America that would lead to a career in some special kind of mathematics. Differential geometry, I think it was. However, somewhere along the line her A turned into a C, and this dropped her grade point average to a number that would put her out of the running for a top graduate school in her field.

"The written report she received with her A was apparently good too," the professor said. "But at some point someone who worked in this office decided an error had been made, and her grade was dropped three points, turning up on her final evaluation as a C. By this time she had already left the country and spent another year and a half of her life operating under the assumption that she could pursue one career that now, of course, is closed to her. She can't go on to graduate school. The solid evidence would be hard copy—physical proofs of this change in her grade."

"She must be really upset!" she cried and her hand slapped at her cheek.

"Well, yes, to put it mildly. But we are unclear whether the new grade was based on new evidence that we have received and stored somewhere—or whether the last girl working here screwed it up. And we have no way of tracing it humanly, by fax or phone, because the original grader and instructor has died and your predecessor has no recollection of this student. Usually girls like you are incredibly good with remembering these details."

The professor laughed and loosened his necktie awkwardly as if to acknowledge the completion of his first lecture in a long time.

"Let me tell you something," the office worker said. "With three hundred students a year—and the girl before me made a mess of the files—this is going to take me a long time. Couldn't we just—you know—tell the woman we made a mistake and give her the original A? I mean, this can't be worth the time."

The office worker looked up expectantly at his gray neck from where she was sitting at her desk.

"I mean, who's to know? I mean, I'll be working on the program anyway, and—if she is doing fine in her classes otherwise—why worry?" she asked.

"Well, this has occurred, of course, to me, but the case

has gone so far, you see, she is obsessed with seeing the evidence, handing it to a lawyer and to the graduate institution that is now rejecting her. You understand. We can't fabricate the instructor's comments and we also hope to learn from this error how not to repeat it. So you need to keep careful records of your research."

"If the instructor no longer exists I'd give her a break," muttered the woman. "But then I'm not an academic."

She was soon left alone in the small dark thickly carpeted office. There were file cabinets stuffed with manila envelopes on her right. On her left a small window looked onto a little court and other office windows, lighted in the gray of noon. She had a large computer with a program in dazzling colors in front of her, and the name of the angry foreign student was scrawled on an envelope to the left of the computer, where her tea also sat.

She tugged at her hair as if in response a bell might ring in her brain. A musky smell hung around her, an air that was filtered through spotty light, violet light, a light that is sick-making but subtle—computer light. Snaky cords coiled from printer and computer down to the floor. She pressed her bare foot down on one and wonder if the Macintosh bitten apple sign referred to Eve. Forbidden bytes of knowledge. It struck her as ironic that she was seeking an original error inside the symbol of the first fruit bitten. These idle and ironic thoughts sidled through her consciousness while she worked, amounting to nothing. She was mesmerized by the light of the computer perhaps, or by the responsibility of her job, but nothing stronger than irony or mild empathy passed through her on a working day.

Outside that evening it was different. Her face was reflected everywhere as she walked alongside buildings. Her hair was like something illuminated underwater. The adolescent girls out on the street, as in Thomas Hardy's novels, workers like herself, were always targets for male cunning and desire. No matter how intelligent and capable they were, there was a vulnerability to their bodies— supple, athletic, less pretty in face than in figure—that made the men rapacious, scheming, driven by a kind of homoerotic (because twisted by shame for someone not fully developed) desire. Androgynous in their long-waisted and sporty gestures, these female workers were destroyed not just by men but by time as a conspirator with the men—vacillation and the aging process—while they lived in dread and increasing sorrow at missing something. Always looking, always arriving and seeking. She knew girls like herself felt that they might have taken the wrong step on the first day of their independence and could never retract that error.

Everyone in that decade was talking about God not existing in the usual sense anymore. God did not engage with creation or take sides or even care what happened on the last page of the story. Existence was now experienced as a calamitous state, an accident in space producing all the monkeys and bananas we have grown to love, and it was up to people alone to mend mistakes and abnormalities, to rebuild the machine from the inside.

The office worker began to wait with increasing irritation each day for her lunch break when she could escape the tedium of her quest—through manila envelopes stuffed with grade sheets, a pandemonium of instructors' comments, ever-changing lists of grade interpretations (what an A means here is not what an A means there), and her assignment to enter and organize all this information inside the Apple. She updated as she went along. The mysterious complaining student (Rosa Liu) had not yet emerged in all the papers, and weeks had passed. How could such a seemingly efficient institution allow such chaos to develop under a series of clever academics?

Lunch break meant fresh air, window-shopping, striding, staring, eating, and emptying herself of an unwanted and inexplicable desire for either love or praise. It was hard to tell the difference. She believed that office slaves are so named because they are a continuation of the economic model established in plantation America. They work for a set of individuals who are unknown to them and are managed by company men, like foremen, who are despised by both the owners and the slaves. In this case the foreman was a professor who had been given this "plum" (a couple of years abroad) for a number of good reasons to do with his academic record, his scholarship, and his interest in students. She guessed that professors, despised by the administrators of the institution, have the same kind of vanity that foremen did on the plantations, believing themselves to be indistinguishable from the power source for whom they work and respected enforcers of the highest social values. They abuse the institution verbally and complain constantly, but this is only a symptom of their comfort in it. People who gripe loudly are rarely those who change social structures.

Phenomenal architectures swelled like stone fruits around her: a city built to last for eons, with rounded carvings, fountains, thick walls, and marble floors. Yet the domestic interiors were like extensions of gardens, seedy and earthy with long windows flung open on the coldest days. The people who had constructed such glorious buildings and efficient aircraft for their last war could not make a warm house, a bottle cap that would work, or a box of juice that would open quickly and neatly.

They were a strange people, even to a person as well-traveled and sophisticated as she was. Their culture was them. For them. Around them. They wanted no other but this that they had formally constructed. They married each other, even if it was a cousin, in order to ensure that the culture remained uncontaminated, fresh. They loved themselves, though they had weak bodies and chins, and made fun of themselves, wrote satirically about them-selves, and succumbed to poisonous bouts of depression expressed in the gloomy weather of their land. They cre-ated the weather that they were famous for: the damp slop that hung over everything came out of their cells. It em-anated, was generated.

She fluffed up her hair, checking as if some Father Midas had turned it to gold and stiffened her in space. To be unheld and unconsoled was awful. Her flat was tiny and green, on the ground floor of an exceptional building occupied by very rich foreigners who worked in finance and politics. She watched television there, read, called a few friends, woke up depressed and prayed. Both of her parents had died; she had no one but an aunt and a cousin who didn't know her at all. She was a world-soul, well-traveled, passed from school to school and land to land, her father an unreconstructed communist, her mother a pianist, both of them suicides. By the time she was sixteen, she had no place prepared for her on earth.

A couple of boys had come across her and she had loved being held, fondled, and whispered to. She had believed that she would be rescued, adored, made safe—but in neither case did this occur. Now there was this professor who had a fleshy tender face, unlike the American faces she could spot from afar—those faces exploding with ego. He seemed recessive and bored, disillusioned with this "plum" he had been offered, pumping across the carpeting, shoes dragging. Often he had stood behind her chair, facing her work on the computer, making comments, his hands resting near her hair, and she would feel herself seep downwards and ask him in a shaky voice about his family.

Finally one day she came upon the missing file and they were exuberant together and went to a restaurant to celebrate and study it. It was three pages of wrinkled and crushed paper, grade sheets, and comments. At the time Rosa Liu was already a serious mathematics major. Here in these pages was the original A and the original comment from an instructor with an illegible signature (he was apparently deceased anyway)—saying "fine work—absolutely one of my best visiting students."

Over plates of Caesar salad the professor and his assistant became increasingly perplexed and agitated by the comment. The other pages were from other instructors in her field, all praising her, giving her top grades, and saying what a pleasure she was in the class. How did this one grade get changed to a C?

"I think it was human error, made before I got here," said the woman, "and we should just change it here and now and let her deal with it that way."

"You seem to be impatient—a bit," said the professor wiping oil from his chin.

"Oh no. I like mystery, the regular part of the job is routine."

"You like it here? I can, I'm sure, arrange to have you kept on."

"Don't worry, I'm fine," she said unaccountably.

"Where's home?" he asked.

"I have none, that's the problem . . . ," she said, hoping he would call her indispensable and make her feel wanted.

He studied her face briefly, then they paid their check and she followed him out onto the wet gray street. She particularly liked the bones in his fingers since they reminded her of her father, whose hands had been muscular from the labor they had endured. Yet her father had often said to her: "Everything is about power," as if his own life had been energetic and well-rewarded.

"I think you should keep looking for the error," the professor said to her over his shoulder, "but don't forget to update the system at the same time."

"That's what I was hired for . . . What should I be looking out for?"

"Probably it's a sheet of comments, like these ones, but sent later—maybe in an envelope still, and stuffed into the wrong file. You'll just have to rip everything apart. Do you mind? The last girl didn't have the patience."

They were at the bottom of the steps to the office.

"The salary is good," she replied. "Besides, I'm improving my own skills as I go along. By the time I'm done, believe me, there will be updated files and a new way of accessing them and a better way of entering the data."

"I hope so," he said grimly. "It will certainly be good on my record, if you get this sorted out. I'm always afraid this job was given to me as a form of gray-listing."

"Gray-listing? I've only heard of black-listing."

"Age," he only remarked cryptically.

She answered the telephone too and sometimes talked to students who were worried or homesick. Usually, though, he did the counseling, and she would listen—suspended on her chair—to his voice in the next room; his kindness was palpable, he didn't judge. Other professors sometimes dropped in and they would all go out for lunch or drinks and she would hear their ironies, their bitter cracks about their work or their colleagues, and she would be astonished at his amendments to their snideness, the way he spoke no ill of others and expressed compassion for people described as idiots and jerks. Yet he never praised her.

She envied his wife and children. But she didn't covet him, she only desired to know that she was respected by him. Sometimes she thought it was physical love she desired and she prayed that God would take away this hunger, and went to clubs with other office girls and pretended to be interested in anyone interested in her; but she wasn't. When he asked her, perfunctorily, to his house for dinner, she went obediently, but grieved throughout the occasion, watching the wife as tall, flat, and serious as a door and her clone daughter as they circled him with critical ease.

One day after Christmas—such a violent vacation laden with obligation and images of the Saint of Capitalism, fat and red-furred and white and full—she went into the office, though it was closed, and almost miraculously put her hand into the file that contained the missing document. Of course it was in the wrong file, one belonging to another student from another year. It was in an envelope stamped and mailed from the northern city where Rosa's university was, and it contained a note from the late professor, correcting his original grade.

I would like to correct a grade that I gave to one of your students, Rosa Liu, who took my class in Theorems in the Spring of 1993. It turned out that she plagiarized her written information. Then she wrote what amounted to psychotic accusations against me, which I am sure she has sent you. It is clearly too late to do anything but change her grade—she has already left the country—and I only hope that she didn't employ the same methods in order to receive the high grades she did in other classes here. Her grade should be reduced to a C, which in our country is no-pass, but in yours is a low pass, I believe. She did after all attend all the classes.

Now the office worker, alone—it was Sunday and she had left her church to come to the office as if it needed her—sat staring into the empty streets. She could destroy this letter, never find evidence of a change in the woman's grade, and continue to work in the office until she really was indispensable. This way she could continue to be close to something she wanted, whatever it was.

As a child she had been very sensitive to her parents' mood swings, their addictions to alcohol and pills, and had eyed them like a little rabbit in a big field because they often behaved like aliens. Their eyes reddened and grew wet and heavy and they slogged across carpets and dropped suddenly asleep. But she had unformed memories—traces in her behavior—of good happy times with them, being rocked, held, kissed, read to, shown to, and the reason she prayed was because of those times, because she prayed really to them in the other world, and it might as well have been God who also liked to hide behind things.

Now she pocketed the letter and left the office and went for a long walk. A few fancy stores were open: she saw herself as light reflected in glass at several points, and wondered if there is any knowledge possible outside of experience. She took a bus and got out near the professor's flat, walking past it, back and forth, a few times. His car was gone. Her own activity disgusted and discouraged her and that night she went to a club and necked with a Lebanese man who was, like her father, a communist and spoke of Trotsky with mixed emotions. He said he was surprised that "a dumb blond would know about continuing revolution" and his finger snapped her panties.

(Alone at home she considered suicide and following her parents to the place where they had gone. This was a common consideration.) She reread the note several times and wished she could talk to Rosa Liu about it before deciding her next move. After all, what did she know about this plagiary, and if it really made any difference in the woman's abilities as a mathematician? Why did Rosa want so badly to find the evidence if in fact it would be incriminating, ruinous to her? She must have known what her crime was, and why her grade was changed. Why did the instructor, in his first letter, say she was one of the best visiting students he had encountered if it wasn't true? and what were Rosa Liu's so-called accusations?

The office worker wanted very much to destroy this letter. But some respect for facts made her hesitate. This respect was a kind of superstition. It was almost as if she imagined facts as bodies that could walk out of the chaos of time—even walk with a purpose—and that they could witness a false fact coming and steer surrounding events in a way that would release a kind of plague of lies. Indeed, out of revenge for her wickedness, the original fact would bend all first destinies into jammed-up paths.

Then she wondered if all this storing and collecting, which was embodied and embedded in the great laden form of the computer, was perhaps driving her crazy. She felt a little uncoordinated mentally.

At work the next day she imagined herself showing the professor the letter and being pleased that he praised her for her diligence, for working on Sunday, and perhaps he would be worried that she might feel, now, compelled to quit the job, having discovered the root of the error. Don't quit, he might say, because now that you have updated the system, you are really indispensable, the only one who knows this thing in depth. You are all but an assistant registrar by now!

Pleased, she nonetheless didn't speak to him but went back into her office and turned on the computer, watching colors pop up and wondering if colors like this would be reflected in a river. She gazed angrily into the screen, then returned to the files, hunched over them, determined to come to a decision about Rosa Liu. Her posture grew tense and threw out sharp pains down her spine, and she began pulling out manila envelopes at random and spreading them around her on the floor so that she could have greater ease sorting through them.

When the professor cast his shadow over her, from his position at the door, she looked at him with the same expression she had given the computer earlier. He removed himself, backwards, and she returned to her task. Days later, when she was still engaged in her pursuit through actual paper, on the floor, he insinuatingly wondered if she was still updating the computer system in the process of searching for this error. She told him there was a basic flaw in the way the institute was processing grades based on illegible notes from professors whose values and judgments bore no relationship to the home system.

"The only way," she said, "to make this work would be to acknowledge the radical difference between the systems and grade everyone who attended and did the work according to one universal standard—Task Completed Satisfactorily."

The professor laughed heartily, but the redness in his cheeks outlived the upturned shape to his lips. They argued for the first time. His voice grew loud, and he interrupted her, and said, "yeah yeah yeah" in impatient tones while she was explaining her point of view to him; he was in a hurry for her to stop talking, so he could talk better. She was on the floor, crouched, but her mind was outside, leaping up the steps of a store with spears of light shattering the time she was in.

Some people achieve mystical perspective on the world by mental struggle, by unrelenting questioning of natural law, of time and imagination. Those lights that gathered around her protectively while she lived and walked were also part of her mind, extra parts. Now she crawled across the office floor past the professor's legs and told him she actually knew better than he about the failures in the grading system, because she was working with it daily. But he insisted on his perspective and on the need for maintaining equivalencies between universities in relation to a global vision. "We would be reverting to a kind of reverse snobbery if we let students get away without being graded according to the terms of the country they were in. The implications would be that we were just sending them over here to have fun."

"If the standards are different, how can the judgments be the same," she muttered, then shut up. She grew depressed. But she kept up her hunt, daily, for some new piece of evidence. And then one night she found it, when she was alone with the manila folders spilled on the floor under the colors of the computer and an overhead electric bulb. It was folded into long sections as if a child had been making a paper airplane from it. But the black email print was immediately recognizable, and in this case written like a poem in a narrow column.

Dear profeser in the rest room
you make me feel your big member
you pull my hair call it part of
the uncertanty world I was just there
to clean toilets to pay my education
but you stole my theorem
but said I was unworthy of you.
You stole my theorem for your use.
You stole it for your carer. Big Phd man
who done nothing for yers. No promotion!
You think I don't know you fail?
You don't care I died in industrial acident
before I never maried my husband
he was no profeser but only loved him briefly.
Because of the one who came
you call these laws of imigration a finger bone
to the one of the word procesor
a stick for the fil clerk fethers for the cleanng women
sex for this toilet washer who wrote a great theorem
you stole and you know the persen
who understans the problm is at the botom
of the barell I used to think
maths could solve anything profeser
but maybe you could help me find a new solution
or proof if you profer?
See no mater what I was respected in my country.
Rosa Liu

Now what could the office worker do with this information? She read and reread the email several times. Her
complexion silvered. She shut the door. It was drizzling

on the dirty glass that looked out into an alley and across into other windows neon-lighted and filled with office workers like herself, facing full into the computers' screens.

What would influence her next move? Her parents' suicides? Her belief in God? Her Red upbringing? Her loneliness? Her need for the professor's love? Her hatred of the professor? The rain? The lights? The light? Her temperament? Her brain? "I'll just think awhile," she decided. And she thought about calling the university where Rosa Liu had been accused of plagiary. She wondered what story they would give her. But when she proposed doing this, the professor told her he had already called the math department and they had been closed-mouthed, impenetrable. But she didn't quite believe him, because of the way his eyes were lowered and looking to the right.

For the next week she cleaned up the files from the floor and noted with some pleasure the effects of her work, her innate sense of sequence, so that the envelopes looked and now were in a form that no other office girl could fail to understand. And the computer system could now pop up the name of each former student, including a grade point average and the classes they took and who taught them, in a matter of seconds. Yet with each grade she entered for this year's class, she made a little change, raising the grade a point or two. Why not? Sometimes it is almost intolerable that order, being so impersonal, is simultaneously so brutal.

One evening she recalled the way God parted the waters, saying: "Let there be a dome in the midst of the waters, and let it separate the waters from the waters." And she felt a fellowship with this action. She hunched into her computer posture, face fixated on the glass as if she were seeing the arrival of warplanes over a swaying horizon, while in her lap she nervously attached Rosa Liu's e-mail to the professor's letter with a clip. She would reveal the results of her tireless search in the early winter darkness as they were each leaving to go home. The professor would be embarrassed because he would have guessed it was something like this. And so would she. And the embarrassment would bind them weirdly as they went up the stairs and together changed the grade to an A. The fact is, at her age she would have a hard time finding a permanent new job.

ABOUT THE AUTHOR

Fanny Howe has written several novels and collections of poems. Her most recent novel, *Indivisible*, was published by Semiotexte/MIT Press. Sun & Moon Press published three of her short novels, and University of California Press published her *Selected Poems* in 2000.

   She now lives in Massachusetts where she originally wrote the stories in this collection, most of them during the 1970s and 1980s. She is the mother of three grown children.